SWORDS & GASLAMPS

VOLUME 1

CARL F NORTHWOOD

INTRODUCTION

When growing up, I devoured books like there was no tomorrow. I read anything I could – especially in my favourite genre of fantasy. I was intrigued and fascinated by the heroics of Robert E Howard's Conan, and of Fafhrd and the Mouser in Fritz Leiber's Swords series, along with many others. What bewitched me most in these stories (apart from the sword wielding heroics, the daring dos and deadly dangers that these and all the other adventurers in these richly detailed worlds) were two things.

Firstly, the differences in story length. In *Swords & Ice Magic*, Leiber bridges the full range with *Beauty and the Beasts* being a shade over 2 pages, whilst *Rime Isle* spans nigh on 100 pages. Tales of wonder for all occasions; the bus trip to work - the long, hot soak in the bath – or just curled up in front of a good fire.

Secondly, and more importantly to me, these were mostly tales away from the pompous, bombastic tropes of 'Chosen Ones' in quests to save the world; away from tales of prophecies, secret heirs, hidden princes and the like. Just plain heroes and heroines exploring their worlds, and overcoming whatever adversity is put in their way.

Here, you will find my tales influenced by those pioneers of S&S – Carter, Moorcock, Leiber, Burrows et al, and their heroes – Conan, Soloman Kane & Kull the Conqueror, Elric & Hawkmoon, Fafhrd & the Mouser, John Carter & Tarzan. As an added twist, I have thrown in my love of steampunk with short stories dedicated to the 'nostalgia for a time that never was'.

Contents

Swords & Sorcery

Brond & Andellin.

1. The Glamouring of Brond Col.
2. When Dimensions Collide.

Sondar K'dar

1. On Top of the Spine of the World.
2. Curses!
3. Only the best at the Shady Scoundrel.

Gears & Gaslamps

The Journal of Abelard C. Grey

1. The Isle of Kola T'ui.
2. Encounter at Port Stuart.
3. The Ziggurat of Sunat Tow.

Tales from the Dell

Javen Silvertail

1. The Triple Death

Brond & Andellin

Brond is a young protagonist, youthful and rangy, and with a severe dislike for wizards and sorcerers. He knows how to handle a sword, but with only a few years of true tutorship behind him, he is no means an expert. Whilst this does make him better than most of the would-be warriors in his world, he has to be wary of the others; the veterans, evil overlords, and assassins. And that's before you mention the dragons, wolves, orcs and other beasts of the wider world. Oh, and don't forget those pesky mages.

And Andellin? Well, you'll see,

1

The Glamouring of Brond Col

He stared. If truth were to be told, then Brond Col had not seen anything as beautiful as the view he saw now. The soft rocking of the ship did little to hide the rhythmic rise and fall of the young woman's bosom as she slept. She was the epitome of beauty, with fair of skin and a face of innocence framed by the golden hair, so common in the Rabic Isles. The young woman, she was younger than his seventeen summers, slept on. And he carried on staring, afraid that if he turned away, she would disappear or at the very least, when he placed eyes on her again, her beauty may have diminished.

"Don't even think of it, lad." The voice cut into his reverie. He finally tore his gaze from beauty and turned instead to the beast. Krodar was a brute of a man. Both ugly and immense. He stood on the other side of her bed, his back to the hull like Brond's, guarding and facing the door to the cabin.

"She's the Bride of Rhaygan. And the Bride is meant to be a virgin on her wedding night. If she isn't," the old mercenary shrugged, "if she isn't, then we are all up to our necks in shit." He took his eyes of the door for a second to stare at his younger companion.

"The last swords for hire that interfered with Rhaygan's girl are still wallowing at the bottom of the king's dungeon. Every now and again, he wheels them out for a bit of torture. That was before ye were born, lad. And they are still alive, if ye call it that. They brought ruin and bad luck down on the islands for a few years".

Brond felt himself blanch. Krodar's voice had dampened his ardour somewhat and he was relieved to be thinking of something else.

"Does she know what's going to happen to her?" The young mercenary asked. He had been the last to add his name to the list next to the job offer at the docks in Amat. That had been a month ago, and since then, the small company had travelled by sea, through the Gold Archipelago and then to the Rabic Isles. The Rabics were several hundred leagues past the Archipelago and consisted of two inhabited islands and a smaller, third island.

"Of course, she does. She's known it since she was born."

"Everything?" Brond's voice crept an octave higher.

"Aye, lad. Everything." Krodar looked at the younger man. They were as chalk and cheese. Brond would certainly be described by most as handsome. Krodar was taller than Brond's height of six feet, broader over the shoulders but most of his muscle laid beneath a layer of excess. There wasn't many that would call Krodar handsome, maybe only his mother. His nose had been broken not once or twice, but numerous times. What teeth he had left were crooked and the scars on his face seemed to etch out paths through his stubble.

"Is she really going to be his bride?" The youth spoke up and instantly regretted his question.

"Ye can't really be that dumb, lad. Rhaygan is a fucking dragon. There is only one thing that he wants with sweet, tender meat like that; and that ain't the same thing that ye want."

"But look at her, she isn't scared at all."

"Her people see it as an honour. Well, that's the story anyway."

"What do you mean by that?"

Krodar was about to give his response when a knock at the door indicated that the guards due to relieve them had arrived. As their replacement took their positions, Krodar turned to Brond, clasping him on the shoulder.

"Let's get an ale up on the deck, my lad. Young and full of beans you may be, but the world ain't all black and white."

THE SEA WAS CALM, just a gentle lapping of small waves against the copper plated hull. The moonlight reflected from the crests of the ripples. The crew of the small ship busied themselves with their work, adjusting sails where needed. Off to each side of the bow, Brond could make out the silhouettes of the guardships that accompanied them. Four pike men stood on guard at the wheel to the ship, their uniform of quilted gambesons in the royal burgundy of the King of Rabic gave them some protection against the dropping temperature. They were among a number of regular soldiers on board, no doubt to keep the mercenaries in check.

"What did you mean back there?"

Krodar looked out to sea before answering. The ale he supped was weak and tasteless, but it was the only drink on board except for water and, of course, the fine wines reserved for the officials of the Throne.

"In the past, Rhaygan claimed these islands as his own, then he did what all dragons do. Slept for centuries, no doubt on a horde of gold and treasure. When it was time for him to wake, he found man now living on his islands. He tried to drive them out like ye would rats from your house. Then he made a deal with them. He would let them live on two of the islands, that's North and South Rabic. The third island is his. No-one from Rabic is allowed to set foot on it, not that they would want to. Except for his Bride."

"That's her, below." Brond interjected, with a nod of his head towards the door leading below decks.

"Yes, every five years the Rabics deliver up a young girl, pure of heart and body, to be his bride. Along with a shit load of coin as well. In return, he doesn't burn them to buggery." He raised the drinking horn to his mouth and took another swig of his ale before continuing.

"The Rabics work it on a cycle. In their calendar, this is their Bridal Moon. Every girl born in this month is delivered without fail to their temple on South Rabic. There they live in isolation, being schooled and instructed what lays ahead of them. About how they are keeping their islands and loved ones safe. The beauty of their sacrifice. As they reach fifteen summers, they decide on the worthiest, the most beautiful. Then she gets put on a ship with the likes of us and we go and put her on a plate for her 'husband'.

"Now, nature as it is, some of the girls get scared. Between you and me, I'm not afraid to tell ye, I would soil my breeches if I got up close and personal to a dragon. Ye would as well, I know. Now some of the girls end up being sold abroad, they are the ones that aren't going to make muster, if you know what I mean. Not like that one down below decks. They are a bit rough, not the natural beauty. Don't get me wrong, I wouldn't mind if they wanted to keep me warm at night, but Rhaygan is a bit fussy.

"They ones that do get to those final years, if they try to cause any trouble, then their families are dragged in for a bit of persuasion. Funny how a mind can turn when a loved one is threatened. As well as the stick, there is also the carrot. The girl chosen, now their family gets a big chest of gold. Enough to settle their debts, buy some nice land somewhere on the island, whatever. Not sure it's enough to replace a daughter though." He downed his ale and wiped the froth of his stubble.

"So ye see, me lad. She knows. She has known that this would be her last night alive since she was born. You and me, we don't know what tomorrow brings. She does and she is facing it braver than most men I know."

Brond sipped at his ale, now finding even less taste in its bitterness. "Why do we have to be here. There are enough guards here to take her to the temple on the island. Why us and not them?"

"Weren't ye listening, lad. No one from Rabic is allowed to set foot on his island, apart from his Bride. I don't know why, but that's the word they spat upon."

Krodar belched loudly.

"I'm going to get some sleep. Tomorrow's the day we earn our coin."

He left the younger mercenary alone on the deck, hands resting on the railings looking out to the calmness of the world, wondering what the morn would bring.

THE FOAMING SPUME shone brightly in the sun, and the sound of the waves charging at the beach could be heard by those in the two small rowing boats that rose and fell in rhythm with Brond's stomach. The small company of mercenaries were split evenly between the two boats, Brond finding himself in Krodar's group. The girl sat facing the island as they approached it. The swell was too much for one of the mercenaries who, green-faced, vomited overboard. The mercenaries were lending their arm to the sailors in each boat on the oars.

Brond was relieved to jump overboard and wade the last few metres, dragging the boat in as far as the draught would allow. The sand felt good under his feet even though it gave way under his weight as he heaved. The skirt of his brigandine jack bounced against his leather clad thighs as he ran up the beach.

From the centre of the island rose a rocky mountain that was topped by a smoking crater. The wisp of grey smoke rose vertically, the absence of wind taunting the party as they sweated in the morning heat. About three-quarters of the way up the mountain, they could make out a small plateau that jutted out from the mountainside. Upon it were what appeared to be the ruins of an ancient temple, columns pointing to the sky like arms calling out to the gods.

The golden sands of the beach swung round in an arc and were edged by ferns and palms. The foliage neither swayed nor emitted any sounds of life. Close to where they had landed, a small pavilion had been set up, with gaudy red and yellow silks draped over it. It covered a table upon which sat a small chest.

The King's Official that had sat in the other rowing boat rose and gingerly stepped into the lapping surf. He pulled the edge of his robes up to keep them dry, his sandaled feet making slight depressions as he displaced the water from the sodden sand. He strode to the pavilion and opened the chest, nodding as he checked the contents and then shut it, locking it with a key that he produced from his purse. He picked it up and carried it reverently to the rowing boat.

"Unload the dowry!" He called to the sailors in the boat. They laboured as they picked up the chest within and handed it over to the four waiting mercenaries, who in turn raised it to their shoulders and carried it to the pavilion. They placed it down on the sand and returned to the boat to pick their equipment and swords up. The official addressed Krodar.

"Rhaygan will appear for his bride just before dusk. You will need to escort her to the altar there," he pointed up to the ruins, "and secure her to it. Place the chest on the smaller altar. Then I would suggest that you return here. We will be anchored out to sea to await you return. Your payment is in the rowing boat."

Krodar nodded, his thumbs hooked into his belt as he listened.

"What happens if he wakes early?" one of the mercenaries called out.

"Although Rhaygan waits in trepidation to meet his new Bride, he knows the word of the contract. He will only approach at dusk. I would suggest though, that you aren't on the island at that time."

"Okay, old man. But what's to stop anyone of us taking everything now, even that dowry." Brond looked at Krodar as the old warrior spoke. He knew he wasn't that stupid, and the question was for the benefit of the other mercenaries.

"How fast can you row?" he asked, looking around at the soldiers, barely flinching in his reply. "Is it faster than a dragon can fly?" He turned and carefully climbed into his boat. The sailors pushed it back out before climbing over the side, leaving the beach to the eight men and the young girl.

"Let's make a move then. Brond, you're a mountain lad. Take the lead and scout us an easy path." Krodar beckoned them to order. At the pavilion were two stout poles that were designed to fit through the iron loops on the chest, making it easier to carry. Four of the men carried the chest, slung between the two poles. Krodar walked next to the girl, whilst Brond took up his role.

"I'm going to miss the rain most of all," the girl spoke to Krodar, although her soft, lilting voice seemed to carry to all of them. "Apparently it doesn't rain here." These were the first words that any of them had heard her speak. The mercenary veteran stared ahead, trying to ignore her.

The path leading through the jungle was obvious to follow and soon started to incline. The foliage on each side started to thin out to small clumps of grasses and ferns and the path started to turn into a treacherous mix of dry sand and loose shale. The four carrying the chest swore and cursed as each missed their footing several times. The path started to wind up the side of the mountain, leaving a drop on one side that fell vertically in places and gently sloping in others.

"What do think Rhaygan will think of me? Do you think he will be pleased?" The girl continued, her face starting to show more than a hint of nervousness.

"Shut up, girl!" Krodar exploded, grabbing her wrist and spinning her round. "Keep that little mouth of yours shut! Don't make this any harder than it is for us."

Brond skipped back along the path, placing his arm between the two, careful not to touch the old soldier. The others had stopped, unsure what to do as the girl looked terrified.

"Come now, Krodar. Maybe it's my turn to walk here. It's a bit quieter ahead at point." He could see that Krodar was troubled and not just angry. He nodded and released his grip on her, turned and wiped his eye as he moved forward.

"Are you okay?" he asked the girl. She nodded and they walked on, with the others following. She stayed quiet for a while and then addressed Brond.

"I hope I please him. How does a girl please her husband? It will be my first time."

"I am sure he will be understanding. Everyone is nervous on their first time, even me!" he smiled at her for the first time since he had seen her, she smiled back.

"Take care on this path," he changed the subject. "It looks very dangerous."

Suddenly his foot stumbled against something that wasn't there a minute ago and he staggered forward. He very nearly regained his balance when he felt a push on his side, though not a push exactly, more of a gust of wind. It caught him and he sprawled headfirst down the slope. It wasn't a steep fall, but neither a gentle rolling slope. He crashed and clattered down the shale, bouncing off rocks on his way down. He finally came to a halt laying on his front, staring over the edge of a steep drop and his feet pointing back up the slope.

"Shoem's balls!" he exclaimed, invoking the patron god of the mountain land that he had been raised in. His whole body ached like he had been caught in a stampede. He could hear the others calling, way back up the slope and he started to get up.

"Keep still!" a shrill voice whispered below his face.

"What?" his eyes struggled to focus on who or what had spoken to him.

"I said, keep still!" He blinked again and went to stand up when something hit him hard over the head, sending everything black.

He awoke to find himself staring at a small girl who sat upon the ledge beneath the drop. Except it wasn't a girl but an adult woman who was no higher than the length of his forearm. Two pairs of small, gossamer wings sprouted from her back, similar to a dragonfly's. She had bright red hair and was perfectly proportioned, wearing a skin-tight tunic of leather that accentuated her figure. If anything, he thought, she was as beautiful as the Bride of Rhaygan was. Except for her size.

He blinked again but she was still there. Was he actually

dead or just mad? Maybe his head had hit something really hard on the way down.

"Are you going to stay still?" The voice was soft but high pitched.

He nodded, slowly.

"Now listen, you aren't mad, or dead. I am really here, and I caused you to stumble and fall. I can easily cause you to fall forward again, and that wouldn't be a good idea, would it?" She pointed over the edge of her ledge. Here the slope changed to a vertical drop some thirty metres high. His armour wouldn't offer any protection for that and he ached all over, so he just shook his head to acknowledge it.

"Your friends aren't waiting. They think you are dead."

"Am I?"

"Are you stupid, or deaf? I already told you that you aren't mad or dead."

"Who, or what are you?"

"I am Andellin. I suppose I am what you men would call a fae or faerie."

"Faerie? I am mad." He felt his head, but she ignored his comment and peered over the edge of the cliff back up the slope to see where Krodar and his men were.

"They have gone, we need to move. Then I need to show you something and then we need to talk." She fluttered her wings and hovered above the crown of the cliff, starting to flutter in a series of swoops up to where Brond had fallen from. He clambered up and stared through the undergrowth. There was no sight nor sound of his companions. He was alone – except for the faerie Andellin; if she existed at all, and not a figment of his concussed mind.

Shaking his head and sighing, he decided to follow her. Maybe she was lying and he was dead already. Once they had returned to the path, she retraced his steps back along the path towards the jungle. The mountainside on the other side of the path was more of a gentle slope upwards here and she indicated that Brond should climb up the incline. He clambered on all fours, desperately trying to catch up.

His chest pounded as they ascended further. It felt good for him to be back on a mountain. It was almost as if he was a child again, chasing his sheep and goats. A feeling of sadness washed over him though as he remembered the reasons he left.

"Hurry, we are almost there." Andellin called, and he redoubled his efforts to finally catch her. He crept forward to where she crouched beneath a scrubby tree on a ledge. He gasped. Where they had climbed to was above the plateau where the altars were. He could see them clearly, two great rectangular stones in the centre of the circular clearing. One was much larger than the other. He could see that the area had once been a great temple, the ground was paved with stone blocks that once fitted neatly together, but now were haphazard, pushed up by the roots of bushes and trees nearby. Five great columns had once held a roof up, but only two stood fully, parts of the others laid strewn about like a toddler's discarded building blocks.

He could see Krodar and the others with the girl on the path leading to it. The Bride was in more distress now. Either Krodar had lost patience with her again or she had been upset seeing him fall. Not that he was under the illusion that she had any feelings for him, it was just he remembered how he felt when he had seen someone die for the first time.

"So, what is this all about? What did you want to show me?"

"First, look out to sea."

He looked, not knowing what she was referring to at first, and then it clicked. The ships were on the distant horizon. They had been tricked and deserted.

"Those filthy bastards! I have to warn Krodar!"

"No! It is far too late for that. Wait now and watch!"

He gave a sigh and laid down next to her. He looked down

as the mercenaries entered the temple. The four carrying the chest settled it on the smaller of the altars and withdrew the poles, casting them aside. Krodar circled the temple with his sword drawn. The other mercenaries dragged the girl to the larger altar. She was now screaming and trying in vain to kick herself free. One held her arms, stretching them out over her head, whilst the other two held a leg each. Attached to the altar were chains that they strapped her down with, placing the links over spikes driven into the stone.

The earth shook and Brond could see small stones slip and slide down the mountainside. There came a sound of strong wings flapping and a shape flew overhead leaving a shadow flittering over the temple below. The mercenaries started shouting, with some of them fanning out to shelter by the columns. The Bride screamed as her husband to be hovered overhead, his big, leathery wings flapping in the midday sun. His black scales shone with an iridescent green and the grey of his underbelly and chest swelled as he gulped in air. Long white horns rose from his head and a wisp of smoke was expelled from his nostrils with every exhale.

The dragon came to a rest on one of the half columns, his claws gouging out great streaks in the marble. The ground shook as Rhaygan roared, moving his head from side to side and letting out a huge blast of flame. Brond could feel the heat from where he was and could see the haze created.

"He came early! The official lied!"

"Of course, he did, he had to. Your friends aren't meant to get out of this."

He turned to Andellin.

"What do you mean?"

"The contract isn't just for the Bride, it's for eight mercenaries as well." Andellin rummaged through her belt pouch and drew out a small piece of fabric. She held it out to Brond who took it. As he held it, it trebled in size.

"What is it?"

"A Faerie veil. If you hold it to your eyes, it will uncover any glamour."

"Glamour?"

"A powerful enchantment, that affects the senses of those who watch. It makes things appear different to those that are subject to it. You might call it an illusion but its far more than that."

Brond raised it to his eyes, the soft pink material didn't completely obscure the view but what he saw through the material made him gasp. The dragon wasn't there, instead half a dozen faeries flittered about. These were bigger than Andellin, perhaps twice or three times bigger. They were also male and wore chainmail. As they danced about, they waved short wands dispatching bursts of energy towards the soldiers. One by one the mercenaries started to fall. He slipped the veil away and Rhaygan re-appeared. One of his old companions was aflame, whilst four more lay dead. He was pleased to see Krodar standing in front of the altar the Bride was chained to, holding his sword ready and challenging the great beast to attack him.

He carried on watching, alternating between the veil and without. The mercenaries soon all lay dead and the Bride writhed in terror on the altar. The dragon alighted on the floor with a heavy thump. As Brond watched transfixed it leant in with its snout towards the girl and it sniffed her. Rhaygan glowed, the scales turning to bright blue and then the dragon disappeared, a human figure taking its place. He was dressed in an ornate, black gown and his long black hair was tied back in a ponytail. Even from the distance away that Brond was, he could see the figure was extremely well groomed. He strode forward, releasing his Bride from the chains and taking her up in his arms.

Brond flipped the veil over his eyes and saw one of the

faerie men holding the girl under her armpits as he flew up into the air. The others picked the stricken swords for hire up and followed the first one. Brond rolled onto his back, handing the veil back to Andellin.

"What in Shoem's name was all that?"

"Rhaygan the dragon does not exist, as you can see. The true Rhaygan is the King of the Faeries and it was he that made the contract with the old King of the Islanders all those years ago. The legend of Rhaygan the dragon was born to make sure that no one trespassed here. This subterfuge was arranged to make sure the Fae folk had access to what they wanted."

"Which is what? I'm not sure what, if any of that was real or, what did you call it? A Glamour?"

"What you saw through the veil was real. Those Fae men were real. They are the warriors of our race." Andellin spoke, but there was something about her tone that made Brond question her.

"They are much bigger than you. Why is that?"

The faerie girl sat down and sobbed, holding her head in her hands.

"It is because they are crossbreeds. A warrior born of human mother and faerie man. It helps to give them strength and ferocity in war."

"A human mother," Brond repeated her words and then the realisation dawned on him. "So, the Bride is really a bride for Rhaygan? She isn't eaten?"

"Eww, of course not!" Andellin answered indignantly. "She will breed with Rhaygan and be a mother to many warriors. They will help to defend the island from the Fomors, the demons from the sea."

"Why does the contract call for the mercenaries. Why kill them and what do they have to offer you?" Brond asked.

"Oh, they are not dead, just stunned. They are needed in a different way. They are milked for their blood and their essence. Their very vitality is taken as an important ingredient in our magics. It imbues our weapons, and our runes that we defend our land with. We also manufacture it into a vitality draught that we give back to the King of the Islanders as part of the contract. I have to say, it is not a very pleasant process. You were lucky that I saved you from it." She added in a matter-of-fact way.

"Thank you, I think. That was another glamour at the end, the man in black?" the faerie nodded at his words. "Will that glamour carry on? I mean, will she feel loved and adored for the rest of her life?"

"Yes," Andellin replied. She stared intently at the young warrior. "You humans are a very complex race. You only knew her for a while, yet you are concerned about how she will live. I was right to choose you."

"Choose me?"

"I noted how you went back to reason with your companion who was frustrated with the Bride. I realised that you had compassion as well as strength. That is why I made you stumble, just a very simple cantrip."

The little faerie woman stood and dusted herself off, storing away the Faerie veil in her pouch.

"Now, I have to ask a favour from you."

Brond blushed.

"We don't have to... er... you know, do we?"

"Eww, absolutely not! No, I want your help and silence as repayment for my help and continued silence. I saved your life, but I could call for help any second. You'll then face the same fate as your one-time companions. No, I want you to help me escape from these islands. I want to see the world. I want to feel alive rather than be imprisoned here unfulfilled. There, I have said it. We are in each other's debt now. To leave this island, for my kind, is a sin. A crime punishable by death. As soon as I set foot in that boat, there will be no going back for me."

The enormity of what Andellin had said sunk in to Brond. This was now a matter of life and death for both of them. If they were caught before leaving, then they would face the same penalty. To Andellin though, a weight seemed to have lifted from her tiny shoulders.

"I have heard a little of the outside and want to see the beauty of it. I can show you where a boat is. I have it stocked with water and food already."

"To me, it seems like this is the perfect end to this day." He said bluntly, rising slowly to his feet.

"Why do you say that?"

"Because all day long, things have happened to me that I had no choice in. What's one more? I can't stay here, can I?"

"Good, you can thank me some more for saving your life." Andellin giggled and rose into the air.

He chuckled to himself as he started to make his way back down the mountainside.

"What do you find amusing?" She asked.

"Because it's not only Faeries that can cast a Glamour. Whichever God made the world managed to cast a pretty good one as well. I'll show you it, but I think you might be disappointed. I just hope you are half as satisfied with it as you think you will be."

As dusk fell, they made their way to the coast.

2

When Dimensions Collide

The old warrior knelt on the cold stone of his chamber, little more than a cell, lit by the sun streaming through a window high up on the wall. A collection of furs lay across the bed behind him. From far beyond the chamber door came the slow toll of a bell, chased by its own echo along the passageways. The chime raised the soldier from his silent meditation, and he slowly stood. He turned towards the far corner of the room where stood a wooden mannequin that was adorned with pieces of mail and plate.

As the bell continued to chime, he disrobed the mannequin, laying the pieces of armour onto the bed. He then reversed the procedure, this time applying the armour to himself, shrugging the chain mail shirt over his pale skin. Vambraces for his arms, and greaves for his legs followed, along with a burnished metal chest plate and gorget. Finally, he hooked a pair of gauntlets to his belt then lifted the bone-handled longsword, appreciating its weight and beauty like other, less warlike men would appreciate the curves and beauty of their wives.

His scarred fingers stroked the blade, caressing it from the stronger, wider part of the blade near the hilt, along the fuller grooves, to the tip. He motioned the tip towards his belt, using the same fingers to locate the heavy ring that would allow the blade to be carried on his belt with no need of a scabbard, and slid the blade through it. The familiar weight, transferred from hand to hip, felt good.

And the pale skinned warrior smiled. The day had come, today of all days. Today would be a good day to conquer new worlds.

Brond took a swig from his waterskin, wiped his mouth and walked on. If an onlooker was watching the young man as he trudged along the worn path, they may have seen him motion as if to offer the same waterskin to his left shoulder before stoppering it and hanging it on his belt. And if that onlooker was very close, they may have heard him mutter and talk away to himself.

'It's fine for you, Andellin. You just sit there and I'll carry you.'

A disembodied voice replied, soft and lilting.

'Well, you are big and strong, Brond, and I virtually weigh nothing at all. You do forget that I also flew for quite a few of your miles earlier.'

'It is hardly walking though, is it?'

'Pshh, I should have left you for Rhaygan - and watched as he ate you.' The little voice started to sound annoyed.

'But Rhaygan wasn't a real dragon. It was but a Fae illusion.' protested Brond. The young warrior kicked a small rock across the path as he walked. He had eighteen of so summers in him, tall and gangly, but several years spent primarily swinging swords had broadened his shoulders slightly. His jaw and cheeks were partially covered with that curse of an adolescent male; the patchy stubble. He rubbed it, irritated by its coarseness, aching for the end of the day when he may be able to rid himself of it.

'Ah, so the human does remember something after all!' A small, elfin figure appeared, sitting cross legged on his shoulder. Slightly bigger than the length of his forearm, the slim figure had raspberry red hair that flowed over her shoulders. She was clad in leather; boots, trousers and a tunic that covered her shoulders but plunged away on her back. There, between her shoulder blades, sat two pairs of gossamer wings that fluttered occasionally.

'The human can remember that the dragon wasn't real,' the Fae referred to the encounter where they had met, when Brond had been part of a mercenary troop employed to deliver a young sacrifice to a dragon. Andellin, a Faerie woman, had helped Brond see the dragon for what it really was; an illusion conjured by the Faerie King. The sacrifice herself, a young girl only sixteen summers old, was not dragon food, but breeding stock for the Faeries to create stronger warriors.

'He can remember all that, yet can't remember that I have mentioned that flying is just as taxing on the body as walking.'

'Shh!' Brond hushed her. 'Someone's ahead!'

Within a blink, the Faerie disappeared, returning to her invisible form. Now that they had left the faerie lands of the Rabic Islands behind, they had decided that discretion was the key, and that Andellin should remain hidden, as the Faerie race was unknown to most of the wider world.

A portly figure rounded the bend ahead, his approach hidden by the thorny hedgerows and small copses of olive trees that crisscrossed the landscape of the island nation of Ardan. The man's robes matched his vivid blue hair that erupted from the sides and back of his head. The centre of his scalp was bald and was almost red in the heat of the sun. A pair of glasses perched on his stubby nose, tied tight by leather straps about his unruly hair. The morning sun bounced of their gold rims as he walked towards them, tapping the ground with his cane.

'Good morning to you, young sir,' he addressed Brond as he drew level, casting an eye over the tall youth wearing the dark leather jack covered with rectangular metal plates.

Brond contemplated ignoring him, but grunted a reply. Strangers who accosted him for conversation, irritated him as much as his prickly half beard. The new arrival halted before continuing to speak.

'You have a fine sword there, good sir, and you have the look of a man who knows how to use it well.'

Brond dropped his hand to the hilt of the broadsword that hung at his waist. He was wary when anyone talked about the mastery of weapons.

'Would you and your friend be interested in some work?'

Brond hesitated, then looked around as if to accentuate the fact that he was alone. Had the man seen Andellin, or had heard him talking to her?

'My friend? Your eyes must deceive you.'

'Oh, come now. I heard you talking and you don't look the sort of troubled soul to converse with oneself.' He tapped his glasses knowingly. 'And elven glass sees all. And besides, my employer pays extra for werefolk.' Werefolk was a term for any magical creature, though to many in the wider world, they were mere figments of imagination; stories to frighten errant children with.

Andellin popped back into view, a fierce look on her face.

'Who says we are looking for work?' she snarled.

'Isn't everyone nowadays?' the man replied. 'But if you are not interested...'

'Let us not be hasty!' Brond threw Andellin a glance. 'What sort of work?'

'Work that I am sure you are both well suited for,' came the cryptic reply.

'Tell us more,' Brond enquired warily. 'And why more for Werefolk?'

'My employer, Origi the Thaumaturgist is paying three silver crowns for swords, five for Werefolk. You will need to make arrival at his tower to the north of Dunholm before nightfall. The village is due south from the bridge ahead. With your strong legs, you'd make it in a few hours.'

'A wizard? Your master is a sorcerer?' Brond said in disgust. His face wrinkled as if he had just eaten a sour grape.

'Oh, really?' exclaimed the Faerie Andellin. 'Then we'll take his offer.' She clapped her hands with joy.

And with that, to Brond's annoyance, the deal was sealed. Directions were given and the envoy, who gave his name as Yab Bey, let them on their way.

'And what was that about, Andellin? I am not pleased to be working for a sorcerer.' Brond grumbled as they reached the bridge, and turned south to follow the course of the river. He spat on the floor as he mentioned the sorcerer, and Andellin made a face of disgust. He continued, 'They're scum, and not to be trusted.'

'But eight crowns a day, Brond. You keep saying we will need money in your world. Now we will have some.'

'But at what cost?'

The Faerie looked puzzled.

'Well, I think Yab Bey said it would be for a couple of days work.'

'That's not what I meant,' Brond sighed.

'And anyway, meeting a human sorcerer would be quite interesting, I think!'

'Well, it won't be. Nothing good that will come of this, Andellin. Mark my words.'

'Is that jealousy that I detect? Are you insulted that I will be earning more than you?'

Brond knew better than to press.

THEY REACHED the tower of Origi later that afternoon. It was a square, squat tower, set in a clearing in the forest. The large canopy of oak and elm gave way to the recently cleared area, the hewn stumps of the trees that had stood for centuries, protruded from the fresh loam.

Among the stumps a small camp had blossomed; several tents and bedrolls were sited around a few campfires. As they approached, Brond started counting the mercenaries who were either sitting around the fires or taking part in sparring with (he hoped) blunt weapons. He groaned when Andellin whispered in his ear, already finished counting.

'Twenty-one, including us. What do you think he needs this many swords for?'

'I am sure we will find out soon enough.' Eager to make sure they received the correct pay, Andellin was visible once more. She had retrieved a small pack from Brond's own, larger backpack and now wore it, arming herself with a needle like rapier that was thrust into her belt.

'Aha! Another one to swell the ranks. Welcome my friend, come and take a drink.' The mercenary who spoke reminded Brond of Krodar, the captain who was in charge when Brond had met Andellin. Although slightly shorter, he exerted the same air of authority.

'Oh, and a Were! The Mage will want to see the young lady straight away. He is desperate for the magic folk. Sometimes wish I'd been born an Elf or something. I'm Kerecsen.' He offered his arm and Brond clasped the forearm in the universal salute of friendship. They wandered over to one of the campfires as they spoke, and the warrior poured a flagon of ale from a small keg and handed it to Brond.

'So, what are we here for?' Brond waved his hands around at the paid swords. Most were from the Gold Archipelago, though here and there he saw some from the main continent. It was a motley crew that looked capable of standing against town levies and the like, but whether they would cave against serious opposition was another matter. He was sure that Krodar would have had a fit if he was still alive.

'He hasn't said, but he pays. Every night for the following day. So, we stay here until he decides what he wants to do. Though we don't know exactly, it has something to do with that.' He waved his hand at a large stone plinth that sat away from the camp, but close to the tower. Brond started towards it, and Andellin fluttered her shiny wings and took to the skies, beating the humans to it.

'Have you seen anything like it?' Kerecsen asked?

It was circular in shape, hewn from the blue granite that was common to Ardan. It was big, wider than three men laid head to toe. Two stones were placed as if someone had started to build two columns about twelve feet apart in the centre, but had decided against continuing. Three large flagstones were placed in a row and the whole plinth had runes and glyphs carved into it. Andellin flew this way and that, extremely excited about the whole thing.

'Nothing, not here or in Amat or Tangova.' Brond replied. He thought better of mentioning the Rabic Isles, where he had encountered the Faerie glamour dragon. 'What do you think it is, Andellin?' he called out.

'The glyphs and runes mean nothing to me. Though I haven't seen a lot of your human magic....'

Brond shrugged and glared at his companion.

'I told you. Nothing good will come of this.'

'Haha, apart from three silver crowns a day, Brond!' Kerensec laughed, patting the younger man on the back. 'Come, drink some more, and your young lady should see Origi'.

ANDELLIN ENTERED THE TOWER, led by one of Origi's apprentices, of which he had three. Four or five stone steps led up to an oaken door that had seen better days. The first floor had three small rooms for the apprentices, and a staircase that led to the second floor. This was a large open room with a roaring fire in the hearth to one side, around which was cluttered pots and pans. Herbs and poultry, furs and bones hung from the rafters. She noted magical paraphernalia scattered about and decided this was a catch all living area for the apprentices - for work and research as well as the day to day living.

Origi was on the third floor. The one room seemed to cater for both work and rest. On one side was a rude cot, with covers and gowns thrown over it. A large desk took the centre of the room and here Origi pored over maps. Andellin managed to sneak a glance and saw that instead of land or nautical charts, these were star maps and showed various constellations and planets. The old wizard was everything that Andellin expected. He wore a red cape thrown hastily over his once white gown, the hood of which was thrown back. A silver skull cap on his bald head extended to a point between his eyes, and his face was a mass of white hair that cascaded down his front. Seated in front of him, their backs to the Faerie, were two hooded figures.

'Ah, Lache,' he addressed his apprentice, rhyming his name with hatch, 'Thank you for showing our latest assistant to me.' Andellin beamed with astonishment at the word assistant. That must be why the Werefolk were being paid more. She couldn't wait to brag to Brond that she was more than just a hired sword.

'Sit down, young lady.' The wizard indicated the seat between the two hooded figures. It was taller than the ones on either side. Andellin fluttered across and took the seat. She was swamped by the size of it and looked like a doll thrown to one side.

'What's this all about, sir?' She asked, wide-eyed.

'Oh, such enthusiasm, Lache. You have brought me such an exquisite one today.'

He swept round the table until he stood behind Andellin. She tried to look up and he shook his head, pointing back to the desktop.

'Lache, if you please.' The assistant strode forward, holding a small dish of powder. He scattered it over the maps on the desk and Origi clapped his hands. The inscriptions on the charts started to glow and the dust rose and swirled about the table top. The glitter sparkled red and gold, and spun into a series of stars and worlds. The stars pulsed with mini bursts of power, wispy flares encircling each one. The planets span in orbits around them.

'There, that star in the centre is our sun. A great ball of gas burning away in the cosmos. And that, there,' he pointed to the second planet that swam in a lazy orbit about it. 'That is our little world. Now, Lache, the next dish if you please.'

The tall assistant scattered another bowl of glittery powder across the charts. Origi clapped again. This time, the dust glittered silver and blue and formed similar shapes and patterns but in different positions. The wizard stretched out a finger and pointed to the ball that he had said represented the world.

'Watch this, young Andellin. There are many dimensions that make up this multiverse of ours, more than the normal man can count. These dimensions exist on top of each other, though the realm of the Superior Beings makes interaction between them...' he paused, 'difficult. These dimensions have suns and worlds too, just like ours.' A sun pulsed in blue, slightly above and to one side of the red and gold sun of their own world. Planets orbited it, just like the others, however these were at a plane perpendicular to the small collection of dust and light that made Andellin's world.

'This world here,' his voice bubbled with excitement, 'watch as it journeys around its sun. See how it is on track to meet our world. This model shows that it will intercept the same location as our own world before dawn tomorrow.'

'But we can't interact between the dimensions. Isn't that what you said?' The Fae asked.

'That's right. Krator and Yesmillia, and all the other Superior Beings have decreed it. They have placed not only the moral locks on interdimensional travel but also a physical lock. But...' He waved his finger at Andellin. 'But, what if someone, someone with an inquisitive mind and nature, had found a way? A being above all others in his field and, well, above all others on the world. A new Superior Being if you would.' He stood tall, his old fingers grasping the edges of his robe at his chest.

'Do you know of such a person, sir?'

'Why, young lady, you are looking at him! Origi the Splendid, Origi the Thaumaturgist.' He beamed at her, his eyes sparkling with a blend of enthusiasm and eccentricity. Or was it something else, Andellin thought, as she sat open-mouthed for a second, incredulous at the thought of someone daring to defy the Superior Beings that had created the worlds.

'What do you intend to do?' she asked guardedly.

'With the assistance of you Werefolk, I intend to force a breach between the dimensions, allowing travel between the two. So far, I have been successful in making contact with those of that plane. And when the walls of the dimension are breached, they will be found ready!'

By now, Andellin was intrigued. But she was also aware that the two hooded figures she was seated between hadn't said a word since she had entered the workshop. She glanced either side but they sat stock still, their hands gripping the arms of their chairs. Their faces were lost in the voluminous hoods of their cloaks.

'Ready for what?'

'To come and do my bidding, young Andellin. To come and do my bidding.'

'And how do I and your apprentices here feature in your plans?' She realised that he wasn't about to be forthcoming with exactly what was going to happen, both in breaching the barriers between the planes, and his plans for afterwards, when those he had contacted were here.

'Oh, you have misunderstood. My other two apprentices are collecting the last and most vital part of the spell ingredients.' He waved his hands and the hoods fell back to reveal a young elf and to all intents and purposes, a young female human. Andellin could now see that both were bound, their forearms wound with glowing rope about the chair arm. Their mouths were crisscrossed with glowing thread, sealing their lips closed. The elf sat impassively, whereas the young woman's eyes showed fear.

She recoiled in shock and trepidation, but not before rope snaked from the chair and lashed her in place. A length of thread rose from desk and stood cobra-like in front of her, swaying from side to side as if to mesmerize her. It darted in and though she couldn't feel anything pierce her skin, she knew her lips were as sealed as her two unlikely compatriots.

'Oh, my dear Andellin. When I said I wanted you as an assistant, it was not entirely true. Oh, you will assist me, that much is correct. The incantations involved in piercing a hole in walls between the dimensions need organic matter to act as a vessel. That is where you Werefolk come into my equation.

Ordinary humans will be torn apart within seconds by the sheer power that is needed. I need longer than that, and I am hoping that the magic that flows through your bodies will enable them to hold that power long enough for the spell to work.' He was shaking now as he spoke, the exhilaration pouring through his veins.

'And once the portal is opened, the forces of the mercenary captain Mol'Tarn will pour through and with the forty thousand swords he commands, I will conquer one kingdom at a time until I rule the world.'

Andellin wanted to respond, to tell him that he was mad and crazy, but was hardly able to move, let alone speak.

MOL'TARN the Bloodless stood on the bow of his ship. He waited patiently for the portal to open. At the moment, it was just empty air, the pale blue sky the same as it had always been. His pale skin was almost white, hence his name. It was only blemished by small scars and tattoos.

Whilst he was patient, his second-in-command wasn't.

'When will this damn sorcerer open the portal?' He tapped his sword blade against the side of his boot. 'We are all eager to seek plunder in this new world.'

'You and me both, Sammto.' Mol'Tarn didn't smile. He never smiled, not even on the field of victory. He and his men had fought wars on every continent and island on their world. Kingdoms had been made and destroyed because of his hired swords. Yet he had grown weary of the constant warring and after his last campaign, was ready to trudge away, sheath his sword for one last time and raise a small farmstead away in the mountains.

That was until he had spoken with Origi, a strange message that had first appeared in his mind. Then later, the face of Origi appeared in front of him. He had fallen to his knees, thinking it was the face of a Supreme Being, or God. If the bearded visage had seemed godlike in appearance, the voice nearly clinched it. Immense and booming, it reverberated around the plain upon which Mol'Tarn had stood.

'I offer you greatness, Mol'Tarn the Bloodless. I offer you and your legions the chance to wet your swords in new blood. Come and stand at my right-hand side, taking your fill of women and plunder. Let your legions swoop and ride over lands new, pillaging and raping. Become my mailed fist, my blade of destruction and ruin.'

It hadn't taken Mol'Tarn long to decide. The possibilities of pastures new appealed to his desires deep down. The legion had taken less time to decide when the proposition was put to them. They existed purely for war, and gambled with Death as a matter of course.

Now they sweltered under the midday sun of their world waiting for the portal to open. Forty thousand swords spread over seven hundred ships. All waiting for his signal. Then the seven hundred ships would rise and take to the skies, swarming through the gateway to another world.

ORIGI APPEARED at the doorway to his tower just after the bell of the cat, his silver skull cap reflecting the light of the moon. He raised his arms to the skies and called the mercenaries to order.

'Warriors! Your time has come.' He waited for the twenty men to assemble in front of him. He looked down at their expectant faces and the murmur of excitement that ran through their ranks. They had no idea why their services had been enlisted, but now stood ready.

Brond craned his neck to see if he could spy Andellin. She had remained within the tower since Kerecsen had led her there. If truth be told, he was a little worried. He had grown fond of the little Fae over the few weeks they had spent together. Whilst he was glad to be free of her constant prattling and inane questions, the sourness of the other mercenaries had left him feeling a little alone. Of the Fae though, there was no sign.

'This is your time for greatness, just as you witness my success and elevation to godhood and tyrant. This day will be spoken about for millennia. You will be here at the birth of the new age, and should you distinguish yourselves, fame and fortune will be yours and that of your line as you become the new nobility, first of Ardan, then Amat, and then of all that stretches to the four corners of the world!' He clapped his hands together loudly as the mercenaries threw their blades towards the skies and cheered.

Brond looked around and saw only Kerecsen standing still and silent. The older warrior caught his glance and frowned. At the sound of the cheering, the door to Origi's tower opened and Lache, his apprentice, strode out slowly. His sallow face seemed to fit the occasion and his dark brown robes sagged on his frame. One hand rested on a large shield that floated at hip height at his side. A black bear hide covered whatever was on the shield.

Lache made his way through the throng of mercenaries and on towards the stone plinth. Brond shrunk back and went to stand next to Kerecsen. He leant close and whispered.

'Where is Andellin?'

The shorter man shrugged.

'What is he about?'

'I am sure everything will be explained in due course.'

'That's what worries me. I said nothing good will come of dealing with sorcerers.'

Kerecsen grunted.

'How the twenty of us are going to take on the world, Krator only knows.' He added.

Lache now stood on the plinth, the shield floating in between the two columns. Origi, quite sprightly for his age, had joined the younger apprentice and stood in deep conversation with his protege.

'I'm going to look for Andellin,' Brond whispered again to Kerecsen, then without waiting for a reply, moved towards the tower. Two horses clattered into the camp, drawing the attention of all, which allowed him to make the doorway without being noticed. Standing in the shadows, he watched to see who the approaching horsemen were.

The riders were man and woman, both wearing brown robes similar to Origi's apprentice, Lache. Both horses were a dapple grey, and across each saddle were two young girls, bound hand and foot. The riders pulled up by the plinth and jumped to the floor, grabbing their captives in one motion and deposited them onto the stone. From his vantage point, he heard them speak.

'They are on our tail. No more than five or six minutes.' Origi nodded. He turned to the soldiers who stood waiting.

'Swords! Swords! Right now, the townsfolk of Dunholm are approaching, and no doubt bringing the local guard with them. They will be here to retrieve two of their kin. This is where you earn your crowns! Keep them at bay whilst I cast the spell to open a passage in the very fabric of space. Once the gate is open, my minions from that dimension will bolster our forces, then we will march upon Ardan City itself, and tear down the gates!'

Brond couldn't believe the enthusiasm for the sorcerer's words that his recent companions now showed, exuberance and exultation. They moved chaotically into order, forming into four small groups that surrounded the plinth. Brond left them, his mind upon Andellin and her safety. He ran up the stairs into the living quarters of the apprentices. Finding that area devoid of life, he ran onwards and upwards. He crashed open the door to the third floor and once again found it empty.

He spied the charts on the desk, small piles of glitter and dust scattered about them. It was unclear exactly what they were, but he swept them to the floor. As he had said on numerous occasions, no good would come by working with magicians and wizards. He made his way to the window and looked out over the small clearing below. His heart sank and he cursed aloud.

A mob had appeared at the edge of the clearing, a large number of villagers and townsfolk, mostly armed with farming implements such as scythes and axes, but he also saw a few with bows and swords. The mercenaries were outnumbered, perhaps three to one, but their experience and skill, no matter how motley they seemed, would be too much for their opponents. In the distance, he could make out a slow-moving column of torches, no doubt the guard that Origi had mentioned. That would turn the tide against the mercenaries. That was not what perturbed him.

On the stone plinth stood Origi, between the two stone columns, with his hands outspread. The glyphs and sigils upon the stone now danced with an eerie orange fire, and lightning arced from the tip of the columns to his hands. Before him knelt the two captive girls, their heads tipped backwards at an obscene angle and their throat and chest a bloody mess. The two apprentices who had brought them to the tower stood behind each one, a knife in hand. A great wail went up from the assembled townsfolk and several threw rocks and stones towards the waiting mercenaries.

On the flat flagstones, lay three still bodies. Brond recognised the small waif like figure of Andellin. As he watched, the electric blue charges flew from the outstretched hands of Origi and struck the first prone figure. It juddered and jolted before its clothing burst into flame. Dark red lights fluttered about the body and above the plinth, a great ball of nothingness started to form. Crackles of arcane magic flashed across its surface and with every second, it grew larger.

'By the Old Ones!' he cursed and flew from the room. He took the stairs three at a time but on the last flight to the ground level, he careened into a figure; Lache the apprentice. Both rolled to their feet, despite both being caught by surprise.

Lache, however, had his knife already to hand. It was short, no more than the length of his forearm and it had a slightly curved blade. Leaving no time for Brond to draw his sword from its scabbard, he leapt to attack. Despite his fragile appearance, the apprentice was strong. His initial thrust tried to catch Brond before he could set a defence. It was all he could do to push his attacker's forearm out of the way and dance past him.

Now Lache was more wary, slowly moving his blade from side to side as he pointed it towards Brond.

'Traitor! You take the Master's coin, then you leave your comrades to fight without you!'

Brond stayed silent, his eyes watching his opponent's hips. Never just the blade, watch the hips as well - that was what his sword master had beaten into him. There! He noticed the slight move, the subtlest of movement as Lache prepared to launch his attack. He was already prepared as the wizard's apprentice stabbed forwards.

He sidestepped to his left, both hands rising to meet and parry the blow, catching the apprentice's wrist and forearm. Holding firm, he stepped back, pulling his attacker off balance. As Lache fell towards the floor, the young mercenary twisted his body and dropped his weight, knee first onto the back of Lache's elbow. Simultaneously, he pulled his wrist upwards, snapping the man's arm.

The shriek was horrendous, and would have sickened most ordinary men into inaction - but Brond had heard men in pain before, had seen men die before; and had killed before. He twisted the knife from Lache's hand and stabbed it deep into the chest of his opponent, feeling it grate against his ribs as he drove it into his heart. Without a second thought, he turned and ran from the tower, drawing his sword.

A scene of chaos met his eyes. Kerecsen and the mercenaries were engaged in brutal hand to hand combat with the guardsmen and townsfolk. Several bodies lay or writhed on the ground. Origi still stood between the two columns, power arcing to and from his body as the carvings burnt in the orange flame. The flames upon the first figure had died down and Brond was not surprised to see whoever, whatever, it had been, lay still. The black ball above Origi's head had grown immense.

Origi the Sorcerer screamed as the magic burned through him and once again, the charges arced to the second prone figure. Once again, the same result. The body bounced upon its flagstone as the fire consumed it. The flames curled higher, reaching the black void above. They danced over the surface before a thunderous boom rent the air. Most of the combatants were taken by surprise by the cracking sound and their opponents were able to press forward an advantage.

The flames that cavorted over the black void parted, revealing the bluest of skies beyond. Night turned to day as the glare of a sun from a different dimension blazed into the world. Brond leapt forward, clasping Kerecsen on his shoulder. The mercenary turned; sword raised but the fog of war cleared enough for him to recognise Brond.

'We have got to stop this! He's a maniac.' Kerecsen looked up, eyes wide in wonder at the noon sky above him. Sun and Moon enlightening the world together. He nodded and pulled back from the line of battle. Brond vaulted onto the plinth, followed by the older warrior. He stole a glance towards Andellin, her hands bound in front of her prone figure. The peaceful look upon her face was countered by what looked like glowing thread sewn across her mouth. Brond snarled, inwardly vowing retribution on any that had brought harm against her. Origi's two other apprentices turned to face them, protecting their Master as he battled to bring ruin on the world.

Mol'Tarn looked up, the sky had rent open with a massive clamour, the sound of a dozen volcanoes erupting. A black void appeared, and fire and lightning blazed around its edge. He heard a cheer as forty thousand throats roared their appreciation. He turned to his lieutenant.

'Sammto, I take it you are ready, my friend?'

His companion over many campaigns burst into a grin that stretched from ear to ear. Turning enthusiastically to his men, he gave the order to fly. Mol'Tarn the Bloodless looked out as his legion took to the skies. It was a majestic sight.

As his ship led the armada of seven hundred others into the void, he almost gave a smile.

Brond glanced from the apprentice to the burning figure on the centre flagstone, then to Andellin's prone figure and back to the apprentice. This one was taller than Lache, and older and slightly bulkier. The knife he held dripped blood to the plinth below. His face contorted into a snarl as he beckoned Brond forward with his free hand.

Kerecsen was already engaging with his opponent, parrying her ferocious attacks with his two swords. He shouted something to Brond but the incessant noise from the portal made it impossible to hear. Brond's opponent lunged forward and he parried quickly, pushing the darting blade to his left. His own steel snapped upwards but the apprentice was deceptively agile for his size and build, and ducked under it. He risked a glance to the burning second body, and cursed as he saw the flames start to die down. He knew it was only a matter of seconds before Andellin was next.

He parried the next blow and swung low in retaliation, feeling rather than hearing the crunch of the apprentice's knee shatter as the blade crashed against it. as his target folded to the floor, he cast his eyes upon Kerecsen, only to see him kneeling on the floor clutching his throat. Origi's student had her fist clenched and she muttered an incantation as she closed in on the stricken mercenary. It was all too evident that she was about to end his life.

Brond's sword arced up and over his head and her severed fist dropped to the ground. Crimson blood jetted from her wound and she shrieked and cursed like a fabled banshee. Brond didn't hesitate, his steel swung again in a precise yet agricultural manner. Origi never saw it coming. The blow cleaved his head from his shoulders. The head landed on the floor and looked up at Brond, with an accusing look.

The flames burning on the stone pillars blazed stronger, engulfing the body of Origi. Thinking it was better to be safer than sorry, Brond dived forward to push Andellin from the flagstone. As it happened his precaution was not needed, as the electric charge died as instantaneously as Origi. The glyphs darkened and the ball of blue sky above them throbbed and pulsed before it started to shrink, slowly at first then faster.

Brond dropped his blade and knelt at the Fae's side. He reached to his belt to draw a short knife and cut her bonds. Slowly she regained consciousness. The glowing threads that sealed her lips faded and disappeared. Andellin blinked and tried to sit up. It took a few seconds for her to realise where she was and to remember what the sorcerer had done.

'Origi!? Is he...?' her finger nails dug into Brond's forearm. Brond glanced over his shoulder at the sorcerer's corpse.

'You're safe now. I thought you. . .?'

. . .

Mol'Tarn's ship neared the void, the darkness seeped outwards like thin tendrils. They seemed to draw in his ship and the several others that were neck and neck with their commander. He stood in his normal position, as close to the bow as possible and gripped the rails on the side of the ship as it speared towards the blackness.

Suddenly the fire and lightning that encircled the maw flickered and slowly died. His ship was still several hundred yards from the centre of the void when he noticed with horror that the portal was shrinking. Mol'Tarn cursed and ran to the stern. There he watched as the slower ships started to fall away as their captains had noticed the failing portal.

Sammto strode over to him, ever the professional at times of crisis.

'Commander. Shall I give the order to halt and signal the legion to withdraw?' he waited patiently.

Mol'Tarn looked again at the maw. The pull of the blackness mesmerised him, and he stayed silent as he digested the situation. He pushed past his lieutenant and stared out over the side of the ship. Eight, nine, ten ships and his own made eleven. Closer to six hundred swords than forty thousand. Hardly enough to take over a world but then again, he had fought with worse odds.

If he stayed, it would be the end of him. And if he went? Would that save him? A new challenge, a new world. He stared again into the darkness.

'Commander?'

'No, give the order to proceed. Signal to all ships - *For Glory!*'

Mol'Tarn the Bloodless strode back to the bow. There he could keep an eye on the void but could also see the ships pulling alongside his. They pushed on as the portal continued to close. The ships bunched together, aiming for the centre of the void. The shrinking quickened and some of the ships pulled away as the discretion of their crews got the better of them.

His own ship forged ahead as the darkness collapsed about it. And then, it was through. The sudden blast of cold air hit him as his flagship surged into the morning twilight, the sun of this strange new world yet to clear the horizon. The smell of dark magic pervaded the very air and assaulted his nostrils. He turned and watched as another two of the Legion's ships burst from the portal.

"Only three ships out of seven hundred!" He cursed and spat to one side but then his heart jumped as the last vestiges of the portal started to disappear, extinguishing the light from his home world's sun. As the darkness closed, a fourth ship started to cross, its bow pushing into this alien world.

Mol'Tarn's hands grasped the rail as he urged his compatriots on. The darkness crashed shut, snapping the ship in two. The bow plummeted to the ground far below. Two hundred swords to take a world. He spat upon the deck. Now to find this Origi, pledge his swords in person and plan the subjugation of this world.

A new sun broke the horizon, its rays illuminating his way to conquest. Mol'Tarn the Bloodless raised his hand to shield his eyes from this new sun, a sun far brighter than that of his home world. As he did so, fear crossed his heart for the first time in years. Fear and a dread so black that caused his legs to shake and he reached out again to the railings of his flagship for support.

A figure stood ahead of the path of his ship. A behemoth the size of a small mountain, grasping a sword. As the ship carried on rising, Mol'Tarn watched as the giant turned to focus on its approach. Its mouth opened and a bellow roared across the dawn sky, loud enough to rock the flight of the flagship. Mol'Tarn turned to the wheel where Sammto and another sailor stood. He bellowed his own order.

"Turn! Turn with all your might - or we die now!" He cursed himself and that charlatan Origi. Focused as he was on the giant's face, he had nearly missed the swing of the arm that the giant was now employing. The arcing arm had already smitten the other two ships from the sky. He threw himself towards the wheel of the ship, adding his own weight and strength as the three men now tried to manoeuvre the ship to a new flight path. Too late he had seen, and too late he had acted.

The flat of the giant's hand approached like a tidal wave, a wall of flesh that stretched several lengths of the ship. It hit, the wooden walls of the ship cracking and disintegrating into shards. Reeling away in a death roll that it couldn't escape from, the once proud flagship of the legion was propelled to the ground.

If the scarred figure of Mol'Tarn survived the downing of his ship, he would have seen the sun become blacked out again as the behemoth raised his boot and brought it crashing down, smashing the remains of the once powerful legion into smithereens.

"ARE YOU OKAY?" Kerecsen asked as Brond leapt to his feet, swinging his arms at invisible foes. Brond stared down at his feet before answering.

"I am, yes. It was just an insect. A wasp or something similar, I think." He looked about him with a confused look on his face. Of course, it had been an insect, nothing more. Certainly not a ship the size of large hornet. And certainly not crewed by miniscule warriors. He had told Andellin that working with wizards would bring a high cost. The cost being his sanity hadn't crossed his mind. He looked up. The guard had entered the fray and the tide of battle had turned against the mercenaries.

"We should be going. I don't want to be here when the

guard takes charge," the older warrior said. "Is your friend up to moving?"

Groggily, Andellin nodded.

"Here, I'll carry you." Brond added, scooping up the small faerie. The three slithered off the plinth, and headed towards the undergrowth, anxious to keep the stonework of the plinth between them and the continuing skirmish. Panting, they made it to cover - then a few hundred yards later, when they were deep into the forest, they parted ways. Kerecsen headed west whilst Brond carried Andellin northwards.

"You know, Andellin? At the end, just before we fled, you remember that insect that I hit to the ground?" Andellin nodded in response.

"I could have sworn it was a small ship. A ship that flew."

"How much ale did you have before the battle, Brond?"

They carried on for a while before the faerie spoke again.

"Thank you, Brond. Thank you for coming to save me."

The youth blushed a little.

"You would have done the same for me, wouldn't you?" he asked. When he realised that the faerie had stayed quiet, he asked again, a little tremor in his voice. "Wouldn't you?" Too late, he noticed the wry smile on the face of the fae.

"Andellin!"

Sondar K'dar

Sondar K'dar, thief, adventurer, and sword for hire grew out of my desire to have a Sword & Sorcery heroine with similarities to Bex of Samak, one of my heroes in The Maingard Chronicles. Slightly older than Brond, with a worldly-wise head on her shoulders, she presents a sensible approach to dealing with problems and obstacles. Adept with either bow or sword, she would rather not, however, fight if there is another way – choosing to think or reason her way through the issue. If violence is ever needed, it will be something different than the barbaric hack & slay style.

The middle tale, *Curses*, is as close to an origin story as I have written for Sondar. Taking place some six years before the others, it places Sondar at an age similar to Brond. In between this and *On Top of the Spine of the World,* she finds herself a mentor who offers the training she never had, and finds herself in a few scrapes and tussles.

3

On Top of the Spine of the World.

It looked as if it was going to snow, and Sondar K'dar swore. She observed the gathering, grey gloom above and then looked at the bowed boughs of the firs, sagging under the weight of a thousand blizzards.

She swore because each day for the last five it had looked as if it was going to snow, and then, to her chagrin, it had. Great flurries of large flakes falling like a myriad of leaves in autumn. The fall obliterated the path and hid every obstacle on it. On a good day in summer the path may just have been passable, however the Feast of Dalakast, signifying the end of one year and heralding the new, was only a few weeks away.

She cursed the weather and her own rashness. What insanity had possessed her in order to take this job? Her hand strayed to her side to feel the satchel containing messages that sat on her left hip, suspended from a strap that crossed her chest. The leather had been lathered in oily wax to protect both itself and the contents within from the intense cold. Insanity indeed, she thought. Her activities in Mandakor had caught the eye of the authorities and she had thought it prudent to move on. It wasn't just the town guard either; the local Thieves Guild had taken offence at her reluctance to pay their tithe. The rest of her years languishing in the King's dungeon or the rest of her life bleeding out in a ditch with her throat slit. Either option now seemed preferable to the balance of her journey through the inhospitable snow and ice - and all for the paltry sum of ten Double-headed Eagles, the golden crowns of King Jeffert the second.

She looked ahead and caught the faint, golden glow on the horizon, nestled precariously on the side of a far peak. The walled town of Hunan Tar! Her destination seemed a world away, yet it was only a day's trek away. The fortress town was sanctuary to all who trudged this treacherous path. And a treacherous path the route from Mandakor to Hunan Tar was. The journey took her high into the mountains that were known as the Spine of the World, a range of jagged and dangerous peaks that split the world into east and west. It was said by many that if one could reach the summit of the tallest, then one could reach out and pluck a star from the night sky.

Wolves and bears were an obvious danger, the curse and downfall of many a traveler. Bandits and brigands took refuge in the wilderness, plying their thuggish trade on those that passed by. Once, she had heard the heart-stopping call of a mountain troll, bellowing out a challenge to something brave enough, or unwitting enough, to cross its territory. The most terrifying adversary though, was Nature herself. Winds that tore, storms that deafened, and temperatures that could plummet cold enough and fast enough to freeze a man mid-pace threatened those that trod the paths crossing the Spine of the World.

"Damn snow!" she muttered again and then repeated

herself, louder still. After all, no-one in their right mind would be near her. Not this far into the Spine. So, when a reply came, she naturally jumped, and her right hand flittered to the hilt of her short-bladed sword, her fur-lined gloves made of rabbit pelt coming to rest on the bound grip. The other hand gripped her shortbow, the string clenched in her hand against the riser.

"Well, what would one expect this high in the mountains. And in the dead of winter too."

The man was young, a few years younger than her, though the clothes he wore were slightly dated despite their grandeur. He was a good head taller, and she guessed that he was close to six imperial feet. His auburn hair and neatly trimmed beard framed, at least to Sondar's standards, a fairly handsome face. When she had been his age, he had the look that would have charmed his way into her bed, but now years of adventure had left her more experienced in the ways of the world.

Her eyes dropped to his belt and saw the long shape of a dirk scabbarded at his hip. A weapon close to the length of her own short sword but tempered to a needle-sharp point. Not a blade to go edge to edge with her own steel, but just as deadly in the right hands. She noticed his gaze follow the movement of her hand, and the dawn of realization wash over his face as he realized he had startled her. The man held his own hands out to the side to indicate he posed no threat. As he spoke, Sondar noticed his eyes glow in the falling sunlight. One shone a piercing blue, the colour of sapphires, whilst the other was a dull green.

"My sincere apologies, young maiden. It was not my intention to bring distress upon you. I wish you no harm."

"Then one should have announced themselves from a distance surely. To have crept up upon a fellow traveler as a cat would creep up on a mouse could give a wrong impression." It was true, he had appeared seemingly from nowhere, completely without sound. Or had she been too absorbed in her own thoughts to have heard him?

"Next time, I will. You seem to exude the air of one confident with that weapon, and one with the experience and ability to use it well." Sondar merely shrugged and the man decided to carry on.

"My name is Harriton Kanon and I would be glad if you would allow me to accompany you on your journey. At least as far as Hunan Tar. I take it that is where you are headed? You seem to have a sensible head upon your body, so I would assume you would be."

Sondar pondered carefully. Several years of trials and quests across the length and breadth of the land had taught her to rely and trust upon no-one but herself. Those same years had also taught her that a companion at the right time and place is an asset in the world. If this Harriton Kanon had a nefarious streak, she may have been dead already, as she had been completely oblivious to his approach. That thought seemed to cast the die in his favour.

"Agreed. As far as the gates of Hunan Tar - and I warn you not to try to take advantage of me. I am no man's woman. My name is Sondar K'dar." She held out her arm. Smiling, he wrapped his gloved hand about her forearm, and she returned the grip.

"At the highest point of the Spine of the World, and in the midst of the coldest winter in memory? The recent blizzards would dampen the ardour of the most ardent of lovers, not to mention the thought of frostbite. Rest assured, the only reward I seek is the safe passage of any traveler on these roads."

"To use the term 'roads' is a slanderous accusation." she laughed, still not sure about her new companion. Harriton pulled a thicker cloak from his pack and threw it over his shoulders, covering the thinner and shorter mantle that sat upon them already. Fixing in place with a golden brooch that depicted a flash of lightning, he bunched the hood up around his neck to ward off the cold. The cloak was as white as the snow that fell about them.

Sondar took a second to pull her cowl up to cover her face, feeling the warmth of her breath as she exhaled, trapping the warm air between the wool and her face. Pulling the hood of her own cloak up, she looked up at the sky to gauge the time of day.

"We should move on. We still have another three hours of daylight left." They walked abreast of each other, neither wanting to turn their back upon the other, trust not yet gained. The wind buffeted them and bit deep through their furs and cloaks.

"What is so pressing for you to travel just before the Feast of Dalakast? That is, if you don't mind me asking?"

She patted the satchel at her waist, hoping that it would answer the question, but her companion looked quizzically at her. She was finding it hard to speak and hear. The gale snatched the breath before she could swallow the air and the ground needed her complete concentration.

"I carry messages from Mandakor. I must hand them to the Senechal as soon as I arrive. Then with those fat golden eagles, I'm going to find a hot room to hole up in until spring and drink at least two eagle's worth of ale." She grimaced as she stumbled but Harriton grabbed her arm to steady her.

"Steady, Fair K'dar. You are already thinking of those ales."

He paused and looked over his shoulder. A worried look washed over his face, and he swore.

"What is it?" Sondar flipped her hood down, the voluminous folds did well to hold the warmth in but also held back sound. She heard it just as he spoke, his voice urgent.

"Wolves. Behind us and not far off."

"Can we outrun them?" She had frequently encountered wolves and their various kin on her travels. Those in the hills and forests around Mandakor were numerous and fierce, dogged once they had the scent of something to hunt down. Maybe, up here on the Spine, they might be different. But she doubted it.

"Aye, if we had steeds and a good road. But as you said, to use the term 'roads...'"

"Would be slanderous!" she finished his sentence. As she spoke, she unbuckled her quiver that sat across her back, beneath the heavy wool of her cloak. A dozen arrows, fletched with white and black goose feathers sat within the leather tube. Next, she flexed her bow, checking the tension.

"I was afraid you would say that, Kanon."

"Aye, and they have our scent." His eyes quickly ran over the number of arrows the young archer held. "I hope there are less than twelve of the beasts."

"If your wolves here are as fast as the ones below in the world, then the best we can hope for is I take down three. Then we will have to get our hands dirty."

Harriton nodded and drew his long dagger. The blade, finely honed, shone in the late afternoon sun. He moved to the middle of the path and pointed to a fallen tree that edged the obscured path.

"Take cover there. I'll draw them out, and you take them down. Aim for the leader, if we kill him, it may drive the rest away." Sondar nodded and moved to crouch behind the trunk of the tree. Her heart pounded and she tried to relax a little. Her mentor had once told her, a pounding heart is a good sign. It tells you that you still live.

She watched Harriton stand stock still, his head bowed, and his dirk pointed to the ground. Then, she saw them. Six big beasts broke from the tree line from whence the pair had come and padded slowly onto the path, their paws breaking the crust of the snow. Heads low, they approached Harriton, led by a large scarred and grey-muzzled male out in front. The other five loped abreast slightly behind the alpha male. A low growl emanated from the alpha as he stared down the young man ahead.

Sondar slowly drew the bow, hoping that the wolves wouldn't hear the faint groan of the wood as it flexed and bent under her strength. She tried to clear her mind of everything except the bundle of fur, muscle and bone that was intent upon tearing her new companion to pieces. The wolf tensed, coiled to spring.

She finished the draw, her fingers and the feather lightly brushing her cheek. The steel tip of the arrow was centred upon the wolf, and she let fly. The arrow streaked towards its target, the ash flexing like a carp's tail. The wolf dropped its shoulder as it readied its attack, and she was horrified to see a fleck of blood spray as the steel snicked the wolf's back and disappeared into the tree line behind.

For a split second, there was only Sondar and the wolf facing each other over the thirty paces between them. They reacted together, the wolf dismissing the wound as insignificant and leapt forward. The movement acted as an order for the rest of the pack to attack. Meanwhile, Sondar swore and nocked the next arrow, drawing the bow and loosing again before any of the wolves reached her companion.

This time her aim was true, and she heard a yelp as one of the pack was struck. The wolf was bowled over and rolled head over paws to end up on its side, nipping at the remains of the arrow that protruded from his flanks. Sondar had already nocked and loosed another arrow and was reaching for another as she watched the second strike another one of the pack. Then the other wolves were upon Harriton, burying him under an avalanche of fur.

"Harriton!" She cried out, her voice loud and shrill enough to send several birds that were watching on, rising to the cold air above, squawking in terror. Sondar sprang forward grabbing the quiver in the same hand as she held the bow and drawing her sword from its scabbard. Screaming at the top of her voice, she struck out, catching a wolf on its back as its head shook backwards and forwards, buried down in the muddle of bodies.

The wolf raised its head and a low growl rumbled from its maw followed by a crimson froth. Its back legs slipped and slithered as its shattered spine sent it into a spasm. She threw her bow to one side and reached down to grab it by the scruff, pulling it to one side.

Her heart leapt to her mouth as she saw the blood covered form underneath, but the feeling of horror quickly subsided as her gaze followed his arm to the dirk that was stuck deep into the alpha male's throat. Blood gushed freely from the wound and splashed onto Harriton below. The youth's other hand was clenched about the windpipe of another wolf, his arm extended, holding the dagger-like teeth away from him.

She was relieved to see the young figure of Harriton still breathing and his mismatched eyes sparkled as she stared down at him. He looked so absurd that Sondar felt like laughing.

"Ahem, Maiden K'dar. If you would be so kind as to help me." Finally, the absurdity of the situation broke through and she laughed as she dispatched the last wolf. Harriton rolled over to all fours to catch his breath, his torso heaving as blood now dripped from his face to the slush below. Sondar wiped her own face, licking her own lips to rid the dry sensation she always felt post battle.

And a battle it had been. Two of the wolves whimpered in pain, one of whom beat its tail in a soft tattoo on the snow. The other four bloodied bodies were strewn haphazardly in the snow, their blood polluting the crisp purity that had existed mere minutes before. The smell of death rose from the carcasses, and she could hear the squawking of crows as they landed on the branches of the surrounding trees. Excitedly they announced the discovery of the carrion below to more of their kin in the distant grey.

Sondar felt some distress at the slaughter of what were majestic animals, their actions after all, had been purely natural and driven by survival; their own and of their young. Still, the skirmish could have gone the other way. The beasts could have won, and the consequences of that brought her back to some sobriety after her outburst earlier. She wiped her blade and thrust it back in her scabbard, choosing to carry her bow 'at the ready' as they moved off.

"Wait." Harriton had caught his breath, and now walked towards the two dying wolves. His dirk was still in his hand, point down towards the ground. A slow trickle of blood made a carmine path mapping his route.

"They'll be dead before nightfall. We should be away from here."

"I know. But I'll end their suffering now." He stared down at the wolf with the shattered spine. Its tongue lolled out of its mouth as it watched his approach, but it was too weak to even lift its head towards him. He paused so long that Sondar felt he had changed his mind. But he then stabbed down, pinning the wolf through the neck. More blood puddled around the wolf and, as he moved towards the second, the first fell still. This time he dispatched the second without hesitating.

"Nothing crueler than lying in agony and waiting for the inevitable. At least us humans can choose a quick death if we have the mobility and a tool." He wiped his blade first on the back fur of the wolf, then on the corner of his cloak and pushed it into his belt.

"Let's go. We have a few hours before the light disappears completely."

. . .

They trudged on, no longer side by side. Sharing a gateway between life and death had allowed a bond to form between them, and they now trusted each other to walk one in front of the other. This way, for a few minutes at least, gave one of them some respite from the biting wind that drove against them.

Sondar looked up. Over Harriton's shoulder the faint glow that was Hunan Tar seemed no nearer than it had several hours ago. She sighed. Harriton, who was walking ahead, heard her, and turned to face her.

"It seems to be no closer? Is that right?" He smiled. "It always does. We have traversed the most difficult part of the terrain and from here in," he paused and spread his hands. "Maybe not plain sailing, but much easier. You will be savouring the delights of Hunan Tar before nightfall tomorrow, that I promise, Sondar K'dar."

It was refreshing to have a partner in arms that seemed to understand her thoughts, her nuances. Previous companions had read too much into the odd comment or sigh, and any awkwardness arising had made many journeys uncomfortable.

A sound of torment and woe rent the stillness of the evening behind them. Sondar shuddered, the hairs on her neck standing on end. It felt like the mountain itself was crying in pain. Snow was shaken from the trees and a fine mist rose from the same.

"What was that?" Sondar stared back along the path.

"We don't have time to discuss it."

"But.."

"I know a place where we will be safe for the night, but we need to hurry. If you value your life, we need to go now." He pulled his hood back up over his head and clasped Sondar on the shoulder. She nodded, not knowing what to say.

The path became less treacherous and that allowed them to make easier progress. Harriton, though, kept up a furious pace and they soon came to another path that crossed theirs and led further into the forest. This new path was little more than a track that wound its way around and through thorny bushes. It opened out to a small clearing that was set about the base of a cliff. A small overhang gave the illusion of a cave, but Sondar was glad of any sanctuary that she could get.

"We'll be safe here. At least until tomorrow." Harriton crept under the overhang and sat next to Sondar. He looked exhausted. He had wiped most of the wolf's blood from his face, but what was left had dried and was still smeared across his cheek.

"What *was* that?"

"That was Myriel." Harriton answered. "She's a winter nymph. She awakes in the dead of winter for the solstice moon." He drew his blade and rested the dirk across his knees.

"She sounded in pain."

"Yes." He paused before adding, "those wolves were part of her pack, her extended family, if you will. She is grieving for her loss."

Sondar stood and walked to the edge of the clearing. The thorns and gorse rose to her shoulders and she watched the trees sway in the wind.

"Will she come after us?" Her voice was quiet.

"Unlikely, now that we have made this distance from her. We should be safe here though. This is an area of sanctity," he repeated his claims from earlier. "We should sleep and rest."

Sondar nodded, but though she was exhausted, sleep was furthest from her mind. She reached into her pack and withdrew a crust of bread, offering it to Harriton who declined it politely. She took a bite and chewed slowly.

"Those wolves, you shouldn't worry. We did what we had to do." Harriton had done it again, understanding her thoughts and the reason for her unease.

"Nature," she said wistfully.

"Yes. It came down to a choice of them or us. They were

driven by hunger and the need to survive, exactly like us. We survived, they didn't." Putting it like that made a bit more sense to Sondar.

"And the two..."

"As I said. A cruel way to go, laying broken and twisted, bleeding out in pain. The ability to breathe becomes a struggle and the hope of aid that will never come wanes with each laboured breath. If it was you, I am sure you would appreciate the quick end, one cut to usher you into oblivion."

Sondar took another bite and nodded. She decided to change the topic.

"Hunan Tar, what is it like? What can I expect there?"

"It is not for me."

"Oh." Sondar felt a little crestfallen. Hunan Tar was to be a new start for her, away from Mandakor.

"Please, don't get me wrong. If you crave the company of others, a constant noise and vibrancy, then you will be entranced by it. Hunan Tar will swallow you and embrace you all at once. Me, I prefer the surroundings of the forest and the wild." He laid his head back against the cold stone of the cliff and closed his eyes.

"One thing, though." He added with a hint of a smile. "If you decide to leave, make sure you do so in midsummer."

Sondar listened to the howl of Myriel and fell into an uneasy sleep, sobbing quietly as she did so.

She awoke to find herself wrapped in Harriton's cloak. The thick woollen fabric, dyed grey, surrounded her with warmth and comfort. The youthful figure of Harriton stood on the other side of the clearing, stretching his arms out wide. He noticed her stirring.

"You slept well. After a while, that is. I think you were cold, hence the cloak."

"Thank you." Sondar added appreciatively. "You didn't stay awake all night?"

"No!" The youth laughed, taking the cloak from Sondar. "I slept like the dead. Now, we should be on our way. The weather should hold until midday and by then we will have broken the back of the journey."

He was true to his word and they made good progress. The sun was overhead when the first flakes started to fall but the walls of Hunan Tar were in sight. A road, this time Sondar was sure the frozen earth could be described thus, led to a stone bridge that spanned the gorge that split the earth between them and the fortress town. With the end of the journey in sight, Sondar was buoyed. She felt lighter and less tired with each step and, despite the fact there were still several miles to the main gates, she was sure she could smell the odours emanating from the city.

Harriton, on the other hand, tired. Every step appeared to add weight to his shoulders and his stride shortened. By the time that Sondar had reached the bridge he was several yards behind her. The wind blustered and swirled, and the flakes of snow started to increase in size and quantity.

Whereas the term 'roads' for the route across the Spine of The World had been an exaggeration, 'gorge' was an understatement. Hunan Tar sat the other side of a chasm. The ground fell away far below and the stone columns that held the bridge disappeared into the mist far below. A moment of dizziness came over Sondar as she approached the edge. Nervously, she retreated and stood at the start of the bridge. The road here was paved and wide enough for two carts with a waist high wall on either side sought to protect the courage of those afraid of the thought of the drop.

She had made it. Sanctuary and warmth, food, victuals and a warm bed were waiting for her. She turned to face Harriton, who hadn't caught her up but had stopped some distance away, where the road could still be described as a path, where he stood upon earth rather than the hard stone of the bridge.

"You have made it, Maiden K'dar. I hope that Hunan Tar is everything that you want it to be, and nothing that you fear. I wish you well, it has been a pleasure travelling with you." He pulled the cloak tighter about his frame and turned to walk back whence they came.

"Wait! I thought you were coming with me?" Sondar called out. The wind threatened to take her words and smash them over the edge of the chasm. Harriton paused and shook his head.

"At least until the storm has passed, Ser Kanon." Sondar continued. "The weather is turning for the worse. I can at least spare some coins for a warm room and a table of food. Without your aid and companionship, who knows whether I would have reached Hunan Tar?"

The wind increased, as if in response to Sondar's words. The young man finally turned; his face impassive.

"I cannot. You go on without me, Maiden K'dar. Trouble your thoughts not about me, but what lays ahead for you. My place is in the forest and the mountains, not the town. Remember my words, it is not for me."

And with that he was gone. He turned his back upon Sondar and walked away into the swirling snow. Within a few steps, she lost sight of him. She stayed for a while, hoping that the wind would drop and that she might catch sight of him again, but to no avail. With a heavy heart she turned and braved the bridge.

The huge gates at the town wall were closed, but a small guardhouse stood at the foot of the immense wall. She banged on the door with her fist and was greeted with a shout from inside. The door was quickly unlatched, and she fell into the small room. The small wood burner in the corner filled the room with welcome heat and she sank to the floor in relief.

"What business do you have here in Hunan Tar?" one of the three guards asked. The sullen tone in his voice indicated the boredom that they faced here outside the town. Sondar patted her satchel and held it up to show the three men.

"I have messages from Mandakor, for the Seneschal and others."

"You braved *this* just to deliver some messages? This is the worst winter in memory." One of the guards passed her a blanket and ushered her towards the stove.

"It wasn't for fun; I can tell you."

"We'll pass a message to the Seneschal and tell him that you have arrived. He will be anxious to hear from Mandakor."

"Thank you, but where is the nearest inn. I can't tell you the last day I managed to eat something that wasn't freezing cold." She clasped the blanket around her, wondering if she would have the energy to move from this newly found utopia.

"The White Wolf is the nearest. Once you are through the main gates, it's just opposite a blacksmith."

The White Wolf, how apt she thought.

"Food to die for," one of the other guards chipped in. Aye, thought Sondar. I nearly did.

"Tell him I will be there, spending my wages so make sure he brings it." She staggered to her feet.

"Usually, the messengers deliver it straight to his offices at the keep."

"If I can walk this far to bring his messages, I am sure he can walk the length of the town to pick them up." Sondar was beyond caring that she may upset a few apple carts. She was tired and hungry. Being so close to town accentuated that now, the smell of the smoke from the chimneys, the aroma of roasting meat rising from the walls behind. And she wanted to bathe. The grime of the road would take some scouring to remove. She would almost pay the ten gold eagles for a hot bath right now.

One of the guards walked with her to the main gate, where a small wicket gate allowed entry to the town. He passed a message to a runner and pointed out the White Wolf to Sondar. The main street which wound through Hunan Tar was wide, but the side streets narrowed and the tall buildings on either side leant over, each storey threatening to cover as much space below, leading to much of the sky being obliterated from view.

SONDAR LOOKED DOWN at the second bowl of broth. It was nothing special - the small pieces of meat floating within could have come from any animal. True, she had had many meals worse but also many better. She hoped that it wouldn't be the best that she would find in Hunan Tar, else it would be a long winter. She had already made a mental note to have words with the guard who had recommended it. Whilst the food was average, the ale was a touch of luxury. Dark and syrupy, she felt its impact at the first sip.

She looked about the inn which, given its appearance, could have been in any town or city the breadth of the kingdom. A roaring fire crackled away in an open fireplace in the centre of the room. Tables and nooks were situated around the surrounding space with a bar at one end. Barmaids carried flagons and bowls to patrons, and as it was late afternoon, the inn was full.

Two members of the town guard entered, rubbing the cold from their hands. As they scanned the motley assortment of patrons, she noticed several drop their gaze, avoiding the eyes of the guard. They finally settled on her, one nodding to the other. As they weaved their way through the gaps between the tables, thought of flight crossed her mind, before she realized that she was safe in Hunan Tar. There was no way that news of a mere footpad would reach this far across the country.

Relieved, she continued to shovel the broth into her mouth.

and didn't look up at the guards when, at last, they stood opposite her. Their purple padded gambesons made them look portlier.

"Messenger?" It was as much an accusation than it was a question. She stopped, the spoon just out of reach of her lip and regarded the pair. If these were the standard in Hunan Tar, then her pickings would be grand. The town guard looked like they wouldn't be a challenge for her skills. These two were pushing the wrong side of forty and looked as if a flight of steps would defeat them. She nodded.

"The Seneschal wants to see you urgently."

"He'll have to wait. I'm eating." She mumbled through a mouthful of broth.

The guard leant over, resting both his fists on the surface.

"Seneschal Kanon doesn't like to be waiting."

She stopped eating and slowly placed the spoon back in the bowl. She looked up at the guard quizzically at the guard. Was Kanon a popular name in this area? She reached for her tankard and stood up, raising it to her lips and draining it.

"Very well. We shouldn't keep him waiting then."

It was a short journey through the winding streets to the Keep. Sondar noticed that most citizens she passed turned their faces from the guards, retreating into doorways and alleys. So that was how Hunan Tar would be. The town ruled by fear, the populous too afraid to be picked out by the guards. Overhead, the Keep towered above the town underneath and they entered through another gate, the black entrance swallowing them up. She was led into the bastion, and then to a fine office on the second floor.

One of the guards announced her arrival through the open door and ushered her in. Several bookcases were set against the wall in between the great windows that stretched to the ceiling.

The centre of the room was dominated by a large desk, with an old man sitting behind it, writing in a ledger. Smartly dressed in the robes of office, with a fur mantle over his broad shoulders, he neither looked up or acknowledged her at all. She waited patiently, then coughed.

"Ahh, the messenger who believes she is too important to deliver her missives." He held out a hand, reaching out over the desk as he continued to scribble. She lifted the satchel over her head and threw it on the table, purposely avoiding the outstretched hand.

He sighed and looked up, resting his hands on the edge of the desk. Sondar stared at him. His grey hair was neatly cut short and faint sideburns joined his hair to the impeccably trimmed goatee. His eyes stared back at her. One the colour of sapphires and the other was dirty green.

She looked inquisitively at the Seneschal who returned the gaze.

"I think I met your son out in the forest. He journeyed with me for the best part of two days."

He answered tartly, and a bit too fast.

"I have no children." His anger morphed into a look of shock as he realized something. He reached for a bottle of wine and poured himself some into a goblet. As the dark red liquid glugged from the bottle, his hand shook. A sip from the goblet seemed to calm his nerves, the hand falling still as he continued. "Do not jest or toy with me, messenger."

"You have his eyes. A pair of mismatched gems, sapphire and emerald. Though his had more of a sparkle to them."

The Seneschal's eyes narrowed.

"He is still out there, isn't he? You saw him?"

Sondar nodded again, not sure exactly who Seneschal Kanon was talking about. She assumed it was Harriton.

"Harriton." They both spoke at once and Sondar was slightly relieved that she had guessed correctly.

"Your son?" she said, whilst he spoke at the same time again.

"My brother."

"What!" Sondar exclaimed.

"My twin in fact." Kanon looked at Sondar.

Your twin?" Sondar spluttered. "But..."

"Yes. Harriton died when we were both nineteen." He smiled as he witnessed her confusion.

"But I saw him and talked with him. I fought alongside him. He was alive and as real as you are now. Nigh on two days, I was in his company. He was no ghost."

"I'm sorry, messenger but I speak the truth. You have spent the last two days with a spectre."

"I don't believe in ghosts, Kanon." Sondar smacked the open palm of her hand on the desk.

"It's true. All you need do is look at my family's history in the Keep. Ask anyone in town and they will tell you the tragedy."

Sondar paused, finding the notion that the Seneschal and all the town would lie implausible. She perched on a chair and spoke softly, intent on getting the story from the Seneschal.

"Tell me what happened. If you please?"

Kanon sat back and it took a while for him to speak. The pause was so long that Sondar thought the conversation had ended. If he had noticed that the messenger who had annoyed him so much was now leading the conversation, he didn't show it.

"We were young, our father had just been posted to the town and it was his first year as Seneschal. The forests and the mountains called to us both and we spent the summer exploring and hunting. You could tell that Harriton had the forest in his blood, the joy on his face when he was in the wilds was evident, whereas it was never as strong with me. For my sins, the lure of certain aspects of Hunan Tar were greater than the wilds." He sipped at his wine.

"Then winter arrived and one day we became lost. Day became night and our courage left us. You have been out there in winter, at night. You know what it is like. The wolves, the noise, the cold." He paused, his hands trembling. "And the other things that are out there."

Sondar thought about Myriel, recalling the howls of anguish that the winter nymph had hurled around in her torment. She wondered what other creatures and beings were lurking up on the Spine of the World.

"Go on," she urged.

"Something was there. I had never been so afraid and Harriton appeared the same. And then the wolves appeared. We fought but to no avail, they were too numerous for the pair of us. I am not ashamed to say but we ran. We came separated and then I heard it. A noise more terrifying than any I heard that night. It was Harriton, screaming." The old man collapsed his head into his hands and wept.

"I ran back to Hunan Tar. I left my brother there and ran away." The sobs became louder and Sondar nearly felt sorry for him. There was, however, something about his demeanour that made her uneasy. But the boys had been young. Nineteen and untested in the wilds of this land. She knew how she had felt with the storm rising, the temperature falling and those wolves padding forward to face her.

"So, you returned to town. What happened then?"

"When I returned and gave my father the news, he was taken ill with the shock and he died before morning. With my brother and father dead I would become Seneschal." He looked up at Sondar, his eyes still wet and the lined skin around them, red and puffy. There was an air on arrogance about him.

"Did you find him?"

A smirk flickered across his face then disappeared as quickly it had appeared.

"Did you find him?" Sondar repeated.

"No!"

"You left him?" Sondar cried incredulously.

"He was dead!" Kanon stood and pounded the table. "I had other duties!"

"You had other duties that stopped you from looking for your own brother?"

"As I said, he was dead. Of that, I was sure." He reached into the pouch on his belt and withdrew a leather purse. It jangled as he threw it on the desk in front of Sondar.

"There's your fee, messenger. I want you gone from my town in the summer. And I suggest you keep your head down until then." He motioned to his guards and waved her away. Sondar stared at the pouch of golden eagles. Now, Harriton's words became clear. His insistence that the injured wolves were dispatched quickly and cleanly. When he had talked about the hope of aid fading with every laboured breath.

"One last question, Seneschal."

He paused, staring at the younger upstart who had stood up.

"Who was the older twin? Which one of you was firstborn?"

"I said to keep your head down, messenger." He swore as she turned and walked away.

SONDAR HEEDED the Seneschal's words and kept a low profile during the winter. Which is to say, she didn't get caught doing what she did best. The purses and wealth of many merchants were lighter by the time the days were longer but not enough to raise suspicion. For once, Sondar didn't spend extravagantly, and she stashed away her ill-got gains. 'Ill-got' wasn't quite the correct word. She made sure that the victims of her plunder were all merchants who shared Seneschal Kanon's favour. An honest thief was more righteous than a disreputable merchant, at least, that was what her mentor always had said.

Before she left, she had one last victim, one more mark to take. In the dead of the night, she crept from her rooms at the inn and made her way to the Keep. In the shadows, she looked up at the sheer walls of the bastion, then started to climb.

The next morning, as the thaw was well under way, she made to leave Hunan Tar. The walled town, though profitable for the young thief, was not for her. She had thought long and hard during her virtual imprisonment over winter, deciding that pastures new were needed. The low country of Ulstaschwan lay to the west, and it was there that she looked to move to next. The Seneschal came to see her leave, his face emotionless as he stared at her as she packed her gear onto the cart that she had purchased a few days earlier.

She looked up and caught his gaze. Those same mismatched eyes, one blue, one green, had haunted her dreams over the winter, though she couldn't tell whether the source of her sleeplessness had been Harriton or the old Senschal. Taking her seat on the driver's bench of the cart, she urged the small pony onwards. She had contemplated on saying more to the old man yet had finally thought better of it. The quicker she moved on, the better, she thought.

Rather than make her way down to the plains of Ulstaschwan directly, she made her way back over the bridge and up onto the Spine. Although Seneschal Kanon hadn't looked for his brother, Sondar K'dar felt she knew exactly where the body of young Harriton Kanon lay. It didn't take her long to reach the small path that led to the clearing where they had rested overnight. Tying the reins to a branch, she dismounted to make sure of her theory.

She looked above, seeing the cliff rise up through the trees. Somehow, she knew she was right. Just as Harriton's spectre seemed to understand her and how she felt, she understood him. Resting here during the night, a place of sanctuary from the creatures that roamed the dark winter. The scream his brother had heard was Harriton being attacked on the clifftop above and then falling to the clearing below.

It didn't take her long as she scoured the undergrowth. The bleached bones of the young man were in stark contrast to the dark earth uncovered by the thaw. Both legs were broken, and she wondered how long Harriton had laid screaming for help before he realized it wasn't coming. The slim blade of a dirk lay next to them, its steel remarkably unscathed despite laying in the open for some forty years. Had he been able to take his own advice? Sondar hoped so. She closed her eyes as she thought of the young man, a lifetime ago, laying here in pain and pieces. Fingers grasping the broken leg, clenching it tight as if to squeeze away the pain, or digging into the soft loam of the forest clearing as a rack of pain hit him. For a moment, she stood still, then she bent to the task. Reverently, she collected them together and placed them by the exposed cliff face.

It took her several hours of back breaking work to carry the stones from the cart to the clearing and another hour to place them about the skeleton. Slowly she built a cairn around him, encasing and protecting him, just as he had helped to protect her. With only a few stones being left to be placed, she returned to the cart and picked a long bundle up from the cart floor.

On the cairn that she had built, she untied it, unwrapping the oilskin wrap around the object. The sword was long and finely crafted with the blade highly polished. The pommel was finished with a circular design of a lightning flash running through it. This, she assumed, should have been Harriton's. The sword should have passed from father to eldest son, yet the younger had cheated his way to it. Her last act of larceny in Hunan Tar, was the one that had given her the greatest riches; a gift for a friend from a time passed by.

Placing it in the cairn, she covered it over with the rest of the stones, leaving a neat secure tomb. Nodding, she patted the top, hoping that her one-time companion would continue to safeguard travelers in the mountains and that the blade would be a welcome addition to his arsenal.

As she walked away, she could have sworn that she heard a voice on the wind.

"Thank you, Maiden K'dar."

4

Curses!

"Hurry! A few more seconds."

Be patient! Her mind screamed as she tried to concentrate on the task at hand and ignore his words. She felt the tumblers click under her lock picks, the faint noises registering deep within her brain.

SNAP!

Sondar K'dar paused, more from surprise than annoyance. A pick hadn't snapped on her for months. She liked to think of it that way - the fault of the tool rather than hers.

"What's happened?" Jass asked, his face leering from the darkness as he leant forward from the shadows.

"It's snapped!" she replied, tossing the broken tool away, and stowing the other pick away in its roll of baize. She secreted it away in one of her many pockets on her tunic. The young thief preferred light clothing over armour. Her protection was the shadows and stealth. After all, if she landed herself in a skirmish, then she had failed. Her compatriot, Jass Darkwood, was of the other ilk; a leather jerkin adorned his rangy frame and a short sword hung from his hip. He was at ease with using the blade or his fists should he need to, the bravado of youth only tempered by a fear of losing his freedom or life before he had accumulated a great wealth.

"Then it's the wall, Sondar. Come on," he urged. "I can almost smell the riches." He placed his hands together to form a stirrup. Despite his lankiness, she felt the strength in his arms as she stepped on to his hands and he propelled her upwards. Brick that had seen far better days crumbled under her fingers as she grasped the top of the wall. Finally, fingertips dug in and she clambered up to sit astride the wall. Reaching down, she took Jass's hand, a shiver running through her at the touch of bare skin on hers. Their eyes met for the briefest of seconds, the same piercing blue eyes that had first ensnared her heart. Then he was seated with her, surveying the merchant's garden and the villa beyond.

"For someone so rich, this Rit Tabant doesn't like to spend money on his surroundings." Sondar muttered a comment about the reclusive merchant. The garden was overgrown and untended with tufts of grasses poking their way through between the slabs of the paths. Here and there, between the living ones, shrubs that had been dead for years still formed part of the borders, their bare branches like the skeletal remains of beasts in famine. Fruit lay rotten and bruised on the ground.

Beyond the wasteland of the garden, the appearance of the villa proved no more opulent. Lights flickered in a few of the windows but the majority were dark. Missing tiles, along with broken and tilted shutters on the windows seemed to be in direct contrast to the rumoured treasure within.

"Maybe it's to convince those like us that he has nothing to steal."

"Then why let it be known that he has a jewel of great value, a treasure beyond the thoughts of normal people?" Sondar replied, the light breeze blowing her hair across her face.

"You and me are normal people, Sondar. I can think of a lot of treasure so let's go and relieve him of it." Jass turned to lower himself down into the garden, then paused. "Hold on. You're bleeding." He added, staring at her hand before disappearing from view.

Sondar looked downwards. A steady drip of sanguine red fell from her palm onto the pale plaster of the wall. How? she thought, then noticed a piece of glass protruding from the top of the wall - a usual deterrent in these parts of the world. Strange, she added to herself as she wound a piece of cloth over the small cut to stem the flow, only one piece of glass on the whole wall - she could still see the depressions where others had been set and were now removed.

Sondar lowered herself over the edge, her final drop cushioned by the soft ground below. She followed the tall thief towards the house. The two stories rose majestically above her, the many rooms dark behind the cold glass of the windows. Jass was running his hands over one of the window frames.

Following suit, she pressed and prodded the frame. In places, her fingers pushed through the flaky paint into the soft rot underneath. She shook her head silently.

"Here's a piece of luck." Jass whispered to her left. "The idiot has left a window unlocked." The sash rumbled as he lifted it.

"Wait, Jass!" Her fingers grazed his arm. "What is going on here? A treasure beyond compare held behind unlocked and rotten windows. A wall topped with a solitary piece of glass. It's not right."

"Who cares, Sondar. If a mark wants to make my life easier, then pity on him." Jass slipped through into the darkness.

Reluctantly Sondar followed, finding herself in a small room. Jass passed a candle, held in a small metal sleeve. A small door on the sleeve allowed the soft glow to be seen, but would allow it to be shrouded if needed.

He held a finger to his lips, then tapped his ear twice before pointing to one of the doors that led from the room. Sondar nodded, and half crept, half tiptoed to it, her feet leaving soft prints in the dust. She pulled a small cylinder from one of her pouches and held it to the door. With her ear pressed against the other end, she listened intently.

"Nothing." She whispered and closed her fingers on the latch. It made a soft click as it lifted, then their hearts leapt as the hinges shrieked.

The rest of the house stayed silent. Beyond the door was a large chamber, devoid of all furniture except for a central waist high pedestal, surmounted with a scarlet pillow. On top of the pillow rested a gem the size of a hen's egg. The glow from the many wall sconces reflected from the many faces of the gem. As she looked through the doorway, a feeling of despair washed over her.

"Would you look at that!" exclaimed Jass in her ear. Clearly, he didn't get the same feeling as her.

His hand closed over her mouth; his body pressed close against hers to restrict movement.

"I'm sorry, Sondar. Even the greatest of riches is too much to share with another. Here, we take our leave of each other."

She gasped; her breath warm against his hand. Her mind was in total confusion. Betrayed by one she loved hurt, even if that love was not reciprocated. She was infatuated with the lanky youth, and whilst she hoped that a relationship would develop, she always knew it would not last. Though, she never thought it would end with such a cruel cut.

The fingers of his other hand appeared in front of her face, and her eye was drawn towards the small vial he held. The thin glass cracked and the vapours rose, like steam towards her nostrils. She recognised the odours of wormwort and sleepweed, then her vision clouded and she found herself falling.

"Wake up!" She felt herself shaken awake by a firm grip on each shoulder. Head pounding, she forced her eyes open, and immediately wished she hadn't. What faced her wasn't human; green skin, a bulbous head and a large eye where a face should have been.

Sondar pushed herself backwards, but found herself in a vice-like grip. As her vision cleared slightly, she was somewhat relieved to see that the beast was not a beast after all., though that brought further consternation. Her eyes focused finally on buckles and stitched seams. The green skin was an all-covering coat that added the appearance of bulk to its wearer. It hung below the wearer's knees. The misshaped head was a helmet, sealed close to the coat collar and the single eye was a visor of reflective glass. Green gauntlets rose to the helmet and unclasped the clips on either side. The face that was revealed as the helm was lifted was old and worn. Bags hung under the tired eyes that stared down at the stricken thief.

"Rit Tabant. And you are?" The man rasped.

"Sondar K'dar." She mumbled in reply.

"Well, Sondar. Perhaps we can aid each other in this unfortunate circumstance that you find yourself in." Sondar raised her eyebrows quizzically.

"Your compatriot is beyond that door." Seeing the worried look on her face, he quickly continued his explanation. "Don't fret. He lives, but he has fallen. And it is true to say, he will rue this day."

"Explain, merchant!" Sondar dredged some bravado for the bottom of her gut.

"I would urge you to heed my words, so that you do not find

yourself making the same unfortunate choices as your compatriot."

"He has made one very bad choice already tonight."

"More than one. Though betraying you, I am afraid to say, pales into insignificance against the others." She almost interrupted him but he raised a finger to quieten her. "I saw the way you looked at him. You're in love with him, Sondar K'dar. A young fool in love with another young fool. You would be better served choosing a new occupation and finding a new man, one who would appreciate you for what you are."

"What other choices? To come here and relieve you of your treasure and coin?"

"Exactly, though both yourself and I know that you only came here for one thing."

Sondar sat back, her arms folding across her chest like a shield.

"Speak on, Merchant Tabant."

"You came here to take from me, two greedy thieves. Though what you came to take is the folly of your dreams. You came for the Gem of Karlan. A gem so wonderful all beauty pales before it, however, it comes with a heavy price. The Gem of Karlan is cursed."

"Pah! Curses don't exist." Sondar half sneered, half spat. Her words said one thing, however her eyes said another.

"Are you telling me that you didn't feel it as soon as you broke in?" A sudden realisation hit Sondar. The lock pick; breaking. The bad luck in finding the solitary piece of glass with the palm of her hand. And then…

"Yes, betrayal by your beloved. I know your pain, thief. My own wife found solace in the arms of another. My children left, never to visit or speak to me again. My fortunes dwindle away. My own house cursed. Only a few rooms are free for me to walk about as a normal man, thanks to the protection of blessings. In other parts, however, I need to wear this magical coat and helm to avoid the curse and move freely."

"Why not sell it? Why not give the gem away or, at the very least, throw it away?"

"Do you not think I have tried? The curse works in such a way that ownership can only be transferred by theft."

"That means…"

"Yes, I once stole it. Now I bear the punishment for my crimes!"

"Now I see why the path was easy to follow, why the news of your fabulous treasure was commonplace. You needed to attract thieves in order to rid yourself of the curse."

He nodded.

"So now, Sondar K'dar. Perhaps it is time to help each other. After all, I have warned you of the curse and what befalls you should you take ownership."

"First, tell me how you came into possession of such a cursed item. Tell me, Merchant Tabant, of how you stole it."

"Is that important?"

"It is to me." She pushed herself up from the floor, so that she knelt on one knee facing her captor. Her confidence was returning. "We surely have time for a few words, do we not? My old companion is not going anywhere for the time being, is he?"

Rit Tabant sighed heavily and sat back on the floor opposite Sondar. He wrapped his arms around his knees as he stared at the door behind her. The same door that led to her betrayer, Jass Darkwood, and the gem that held a curse.

"A dozen years ago, I received word from an old adversary, a competitor if you may. He had fallen on, or so he claimed, hard times. Sensing a killing," he paused, seeing the shock on her face at his words. "I meant a metaphorical killing. Perhaps I could purchase parts of his business under their value. It was evident as soon as I had arrived that he had been telling the truth. His mansion was close to ruin and his wife was just as close to leaving him. After negotiating a price more to my liking..."

"An unfair price, do you mean?" spat Sondar interrupting the older man. He reddened, and Sondar knew that he had borne a heavy price for his actions. He slowly nodded, his arms closing tightly about his knees as he carried on.

"Yes, if you say. An unfair price. Afterwards, that very night, I took advantage of his wife. She wanted to trade a secret for a way out of her miserable marriage."

"The gem?" Sondar interrupted again, this time with a little less venom in her tone.

"Yes. As she lay in my arms, she mentioned a gem that her husband gazed upon for hours every day. A treasure that, despite the dilapidation of his home, he was loath to part with. And so, I betrayed them both; a broken promise to take her with me when I left. And with him, a triple cut of treachery. I had taken his wife, then paid a pittance for his businesses, and finally," he closed his eyes as he thought back to the moment that brought his life crashing down. "Finally, I stole into his chamber that very night and stripped him of the gem." He stood and adjusted his magical coat. He held his hands out wide and looked from side to side, indicating the house and his life. "And this is what I gained from my actions."

Sondar could only nod. The merchant's face sank, his eyes almost lifeless despite the possibility of the curse being lifted. He reached down to her, a hand outstretched ready to take hers.

"What do you need me to do?"

"Return to your ex-compatriot. Help him to the other door and hence to the boundary of the grounds. Then, you are free to go. No city guards or reputation to follow you. Just refuse to return to his side if he asks. That way you are not party to the theft, and also, I am not party in his escape, hence both of us avoiding the curse."

He still held out his hand towards her, and Sondar grasped it, surprised by the grip of the old man. She pulled herself to her feet. Tentatively, she moved to the door, her hand reaching out to clasp the cold metal of the handle. As she opened it, she stole a glance behind her. Rit Tabant looked up at her, his eyes pleading with her to do as he asked.

In the next chamber, she found Jass sitting with his back against the pedestal. The scarlet pillow was empty. On seeing Sondar, Jass dropped one hand to his sword hilt, the other clasped a pouch on his belt.

"What happened to you?" she asked.

"Slipped on this floor. I just can't believe my luck. Anyway, keep back. I may have sprained my ankle, but I could still take you in a fight."

Her eyes fell on his ankle and the unnatural way the foot angled away from his leg. That was no sprain she thought. But Jass, being Jass, would swear all day that it was but a sprain or just a scratch, never anything worse. She decided not to push further.

"I haven't come here to fight, Jass. I just want to show you the way out."

"Really!" He didn't believe her.

"Yes, come on. Let me help you up."

"Stay your hand, Sondar. If you try to take it, I will hunt you down. Believe me."

Sondar K'dar looked down upon the man who had betrayed her, a man who had shunned her, then cheated her and left her to be captured. All for riches. She looked back over her shoulder, and stared at the door from whence she came. Sondar imagined the figure standing behind, the green coat swamping his thin figure, the helmet with its singular, central eye staring back at her through the oaken panels of the door.

The merchant waiting patiently for his imprisonment to end. A man who had preyed upon the desires and weaknesses of others in order to increase his once obscene wealth.

A choice needed to be made. She felt the hairs on the back of her neck stand up on end. Whether that was the proximity of the Gem of Karlan, or the eyes of Tabant burning through the door into her mind, she did not know. Could she trust the merchant not to inform the city guard about her once the curse was lifted? He had, even in his own words, a perchance for betrayal. Her eyes fell on Jass, who was trying to clamber to his one good foot. The focus of her attention over the last few months was just a spurner and a treacherous one at that.

She looked up, and noticed the door at the far end of the chamber. A small stained-glass circle was sat towards the top of the door, the coloured segments forming a sun bursting from behind a mountain. Slowly, as she watched, the glass ignited, as the breaking sun beyond cast a beam towards the base of the pedestal that the gem had once sat upon.

"Daybreak," she announced. "A new day is dawning!" Without a backward glance, she strode towards the light. She had made her choice.

5

Only the Best at the Shady Scoundrel.

Sondar K'dar cursed the storm and reached for the inn door. A weather-beaten sign hung above her, creaking in the wind. It depicted a cloaked and hooded figure, with its features obscured. Some indecipherable runes ran vertically down one side of the figure. As her fingers sought the blackened latch, a cascade of water fell from the porch tiles above, the cold water inevitably finding the gap between her oilskin coat and the skin at the nape of her neck. She stifled a shriek and spewed forth a few more curses, aimed at the weather, the plains of Ulstaschwan (where she found herself to be), and finally at herself for deciding the aforesaid plains were a suitable location to travel. Though, no matter how sodden the plains were with the customary summer rainfall, she had to admit they were a better prospect than her previous stay at Hunan Tar.

A much better prospect indeed, than the town on top of the

Spine of the World. The walled town of Hunan Tar had offered a refuge over the winter, but she had outlived the welcome of the townsfolk and their seneschal in those few months. As her mentor had drummed into her at a young age, all authorities have a habit of catching up with thieves and it would only be a matter of time before she fell afoul of the town guard, as inept as they were.

"There are old thieves, and there are bold thieves, but there are no old, bold thieves," she muttered to herself as she clicked the latch and pushed her way across the threshold and into the inn. A blast of heat welcomed her along with the aroma of a hearty stew that bubbled away on the hearth. A wisp of a child stirred the pan with a ladle, the handle wrapped in cloth to protect from the heat.

As she shook the rain from her coat she took in the rest of the inn and its occupants. On her left was a bar that ran the length of the room, behind whom stood the innkeeper. A stained apron covered his portly waist. His face was a mess of scars, which Sondar took to be evidence of a more dangerous occupation before he took the inn, maybe sinking his savings as a soldier or sword for hire into the establishment. Either that, or the clientele found on the plains of Ulstaschwan were more dangerous than she thought.

A soldier sat with his back to the far wall, his hands drawing a whetstone along the blade of his longsword. The steel sang as the stone honed the edge of the blade. His chainmail hauberk was mostly covered by a surcoat emblazoned with an image of a rampant black wolf. He looked up, his eyes meeting hers for the briefest of time then they seemed to flick across her, taking in the various weapons that were strapped to her body; the short bow strapped across her back, the falchion at her waist and the two daggers thrust into the top of her boots.

He swished the whetstone along the edge of the blade once

more and gave a slight nod of what Sondar took to be grudging approval. Whether it was her arms or charms that he approved of was of no concern to the slight thief. With his hooked nose and unshaven appearance, he wasn't her type, and the razor-sharp blades of her twin companions that were pushed into the collar of her boots would reinforce that if needed. She glanced around, taking in the other occupants.

Seated about the hearth were several others. A well-groomed man, who bore the same emblem as the soldier tending to his sword, sat on a wooden chair. Its high, hard back lent an air of elegance to his authority. This was a man used to better surroundings than this, possibly a captain or higher rank, and from a well-to-do family or whatever passed for nobility in his area of the world. His dark beard was flecked with grey, yet his eyes had a youthful appeal to them. His fingers curled suggestively around the bowl of a goblet of wine.

Somewhat older, the next patron was curled up in a small booth, a bowlful of the steaming stew sat on the table next to a pile of dusty and worn tomes, their leather covers adorned with brass findings and trimmings and inscribed with runes and other symbols. He looked as dusty and worn as his books, his straggly hair totally grey, matching the unkempt beard that flowed to his chest. The robes he wore had seen better days as well, the original sandy colour nearly obliterated by stains of every bit of terrain from here to the coast. One hand rested upon the books, the other fidgeted with the spoon that sat in the bowl.

Next, a giant of a man sat on a stool, resting his tree trunk-like arms on an ale-soaked table. A giant in all measurements except that of height. Immense shoulders topped a barrel chest, which Sondar would have attributed to a lifetime of lifting and carrying, if it wasn't for the heavy gut underneath. Years of good eating had given the man a rosy complexion, his pockmarked and scarred face as red as the wine in the flagon he nursed between the fingers of his ham-like fists. A medallion in the shape of a golden sun hung from a cord around his neck, sitting brightly against the dark umber hue of his garments. A heavy staff was propped precariously against the table, its shaft as thick as Sondar's forearm, each end capped in iron. For all its weight and thickness, though, it would look as slender as a javelin in his thickset hands.

All looked up from their drinks or ruminations at the disturbance of her entrance. The wind howling from outside had heralded her appearance as she pushed the door shut behind her. None of the four uttered a word and it was left to the fifth patron to verbally welcome her.

"At last, the storm has delivered another glowing gemstone to this desperate, forsaken corner of the country, in recompense for the earlier delivery of four rancid and boring turds." The speaker raised a flagon towards her from his vantage point at the far end of the bar. Perched upon a tall stool, he had mousey, foppish hair that framed a youthful face, though he still appeared to have a few summers more than her twenty-two. His mouth split open in a grin, revealing an almost perfect set of teeth, marred by a missing incisor. The black gap seemed to add to his boyish charm. A naked sword was thrust through the belt at his hip, a belt that clamped the waist of the too large leather jerkin around his slender figure.

"Barkeep! Another of your finest ales, good sir, and one made from week old dishwater for our new companion." He leant forward, as if to be seen to address her surreptitiously. "Don't worry, they are one and the same. Only the best in *The Shady Scoundrel!*"

The barman mumbled something in reply, the sound hardly carrying past his pursed and cracked lips.

"I pay for my own ale, if you don't mind. At least until friendship is proven." Sondar replied, reaching for her coin purse at her hip. The snub seemed to wash over the man, who carried on.

"Should there be no doubt as to who I referred to in my earlier reference, I, of course, am the earlier gem to have been washed down to this barely adequate establishment. The boorish turds, however..." He spread his arms, as if to embrace the other four patrons.

"You should keep your tongue still, boy." The well-groomed man spoke, one hand placing the goblet on the table before him, whilst the other tightened about the arm of his chair. "If ceaseless prattle was a crime in these parts, I would have hung you four times over this very evening!"

"The first time, I would have welcomed, if only to escape the boredom. The other three times, I would have endured them as well, though the fourth may well have proven tiresome." The young man spoke again, raising his now full flagon to his seated fellows in a salute. The barman placed a flagon on the bar in front of Sondar, the weak brown liquid sloshing over the rim of the wooden vessel. He snatched the coin that she had deposited onto the bar. She picked up the ale, and started to navigate her way towards the fire, making for a solitary stool that would place her within the warming embrace of the glowing coals and logs.

"Enough!" growled the giant, his voice rumbling like thunder. "You do not know the reason for my journey, the fears and trials I will have to face in order to succeed."

"Oh, I do. I know the reason well enough. I know yours," the young man answered, jabbing a finger towards the giant, then at the old man in the booth and the well-groomed man who Sondar now found herself seated close to. "And yours, and yours. Because it is the same as mine. We seek the same result, but the 'why' is different for each of us."

"Pah!" rumbled the giant. "You know nothing!"

"It is easy enough to deduce. Even a blind outsider could

guess. You, there!" He pointed to Sondar. "Tell us why we are here."

Sondar shook her head, her oilskin coat now peeled off and laying over a stool in front of the fire. She sipped her ale, the description the young man had been correct. Weak and willing, it tasted of nothing as it went down.

"It is not my business. I am just passing through."

"And pass on you should, right now. This is no place for a young maiden, even if she believes she could hold her own." The bearded man with the black wolf emblazoned on his tunic glared at her, his goblet rising towards his lips.

Really, thought Sondar. This inn, the so-called *Shady Scoundrel* had been the first sign of habitation she had seen for miles. To leave and endure the storm outside would be madness, no matter what those inside thought.

"I'll bite." She stood and downed the weak ale. Throwing the empty flagon to the young man at the bar, she snapped. "Now I'll take that ale you offered." She stared at each one.

The grey-haired man in the booth had taken a pipe to hand and had packed it with foul smelling weed from a pouch. Well-travelled, no time to wash or clean oneself. Books and tomes indicated a clerk, however, books and tomes with runes and symbols told another story. He clicked his fingers, a small flame appearing between thumb and forefinger. He applied the flame to the weed in the bowl of the pipe, the hand holding the ornate ceramic shaking as he did so.

Next, the giant. The sun medallion told Sondar that he was following the Child of the Light, the new god from the south. His weight and complexion showed a measure of ill-health, perhaps a final chance of absolution.

The two soldiers; the captain and the guard. Now he had spoken, she placed the captain's accent to be from the north, the wolf possibly an emblem of one of the jarldoms in the mountains. Two together gave an alternative to her first suspicion.

Finally, the young man. Cocky and arrogant, the quickfire mouth a false sense of bravado. Ill-prepared with ill-fitting armour and a sword with no sheath. Their appearances taken singularly could mean anything yet taken as a whole allowed Sondar to piece together a narrative. She pointed to the man in the booth.

"You have travelled far and fast. You have had no time to care for yourself, so you are pressed for time, and your hands shake. You are scared. Scared of what is behind you, or in front of you. At first, I thought you were fleeing from something or someone, but then," she turned to the giant. "You follow the Child of the Light. A god that requires his followers to carry out quests in order to admonish previous sins, such as years of good living to excess. One final chance to gather favour with your god. You are on a quest, to do just that, running towards something."

"Confirmed by your presence." She nodded towards the captain. "From the mountains, this far south, far from home. Beyond your normal jurisdiction but two of you, so not fleeing, but hunting or chasing something. Something or someone dangerous. Which leads us to you." She turned and pointed at the young man.

"You are no warrior. That jerkin is not yours and that sword has seen better days. Ill-prepared or harnessed in haste. You are more scared than you let on, mainly because you have seen what you chase or what it can do. Your reason, I know. Revenge." He blanched, turning white as she spoke. He handed the flagon to the barkeep, who mumbled incoherently. "You all chase something, which has led you here. Whether it is the same thing or different, I know not."

"You have a good eye." The grey-haired man spoke, taking a

puff on his pipe. Bitter smoke rose towards the ceiling, and he gave an inquisitive look at Sondar.

"Sondar, Sondar K'dar." She guessed he was inquiring as to who she was.

"Well, Sondar. You are right with your deductions, at least where I am concerned. I am Storn, an apprentice mage, from Albarny in the west. My master, the Warlock Yan Tar, pressed upon me a geas that needs to be completed afore the next double moon. A monster is roaming the land and he wants a vial of its blood for his studies. It is also an examination of my skills as a mage, my first test on my own." He puffed a ring of smoke from the bowl of the pipe.

"Again, correct in your surmise." The well-groomed man spoke, placing the goblet in front of him. He stood and slowly lowered his head a few inches in an informal bow. "Prosecutor Smit. I have been tasked by my liege lord, Jarl Enrik dei Wolfe, along with Callan here," he indicated the seated soldier, "to apprehend a violent murderer who has laid waste to many a farmstead on the borders of his lands. Our trail leads here."

The giant spoke, his voice harsh and foreboding. He raised a hand to scratch the stubble of his shaven head as the words tumbled from his mouth.

"I am indeed an acolyte of the Child. I now go by the name of Garith. My Pastor Shepherd bade me on this quest to rid the land of an evil beast. One that attacked a church a few moons ago and killed many. I must prove myself worthy of a place in the Hall of the Light."

They all turned to stare at the foppish youngster. He stared back, blushing furiously as he fought back tears. He downed the pint of ale he held, the one intended for Sondar, then turned and requested another from the barman.

"It came into our house one night; I was working the fields late when I heard the screams. I rushed back, not knowing what I would find; then I saw it. It was a thing from Hel, an abomination of teeth and spikes and claws. I saw, I saw what it had done to my family, to my wife and son. To my poor Elen and Jon." He stared blankly at the far wall, staring through them as if he was the sole patron in the inn. "I stood, paralyzed with fear as it turned and looked at me. Then it was gone. It took me a day to bury them. And then I vowed, 'Jontie, I said to myself. Find it and kill it. Or die trying."

He paled, and sat down again, his body racked by a huge sob.

Sondar stood and approached the young girl stirring the stew at the hearth. She motioned for a bowl, enquiring how much. The youth smiled, her teeth crooked and stained. Like her father, she mumbled something unintelligible in response. Sondar dug her fingers into her coin purse, pulling out a pair of copper crowns. She hoped that it would be enough, though the thought of the weather outside made any price for the stew reasonable. Swapping the coins for a wooden bowl, the young server ladled out lumps of meat and vegetables.

"Very good, Maiden K'dar. You seem to have picked us all. Though your theory that we could all be seeking the same miscreant is absurd." Prosecutor Smit rubbed the knuckles of one hand with the fingers of the other, his eyes fixed upon Sondar.

"A mere possibility, no more. I was asked for my assumption, and I gave it. Unwillingly as well, I may add."

"Still, our quarry is human, though the state of his mind may be more animal in nature. From the wounds upon the victims left in his wake, he has a penchant for twin blades." His eyes dropped to her boots. "Or she has."

"What are you implying?" seethed Sondar, trying desperately to keep herself under control. She forced herself to take another mouthful of stew.

"Nothing at all. I was just answering your assumption with one of my own. 'Passing through' and you happen to be right here. A strange coincidence considering out trail had gone quiet until several days ago when we were given this inn as a reference point to start afresh."

Before Sondar could answer the accusation, Garith the acolyte stood, his imposing presence forming a barrier between Smit and Sondar.

"You say you were told to seek this inn out?"

"Yes, what of it, Acolyte."

"You spoke of coincidences. I, too, was directed to seek out the *Shady Scoundrel*. My trail had similarly gone cold."

"You too?" Jontie jumped down from the bar stool that he had perched himself upon. His tears had subsided, but his eyes still were red and swollen.

"All four of us, it would appear." Storn the mage sat forward; the bowl of his pipe sat in his hands as he addressed the rest.

"All four of you were directed to start your search anew, here? And you only just talk about it now? By whom?" Sondar said incredulously. The four stood slightly abashed.

"A man by the ford on the River Ux." Jontie was first to answer.

"And what did he look like?" Sondar asked.

Jontie brow furrowed, then his face reddened more.

"Now, that is the oddest thing. I cannot remember at all."

"Nothing at all?" inquired the Prosecutor, turning to the young man, the hint of a sneer in his voice.

"What about you then? Can you do better?" Jontie snapped back.

"Of course! I am the best Prosecutor in the jarldom!" His face went blank. He turned, almost imploringly to Callan. The guard's face was as empty as his captain's.

"A man. That is all I can remember." He stammered out, ashamed that he had caused embarrassment to his superior.

Storn and Garith fared no better in delving into their memories.

"One thing, though. It was only by chance that I found the inn." The wizard's apprentice said. "Most I spoke to had never heard of it. Strange, as it is evidently old and is close to the main path through the plains."

"Aye," interjected Smit, his hand rubbing his greying beard. "The same, though I took the lack of directions to be a stand against authority. I have found no one likes to volunteer information to a Prosecutor."

"Maybe it is known by another name locally?" added the hefty acolyte.

The door crashed open with a huge thud, the hinges jarring as it struck the wall. A blast of cold air and spray from the rain invaded the warm interior of the inn. A true giant of a figure stooped to enter, his form filling the doorway and providing a barrier to the wind.

Clad in furs and a plate breastplate that would have appeared loose on the barrel-chested Garith, the figure glared at them. Dark brown eyes set within the green skin of an orc. White hair flowing over the bearskin mantle that sat upon his shoulders, his eyes scanned the room, taking in each one in turn. In his hand was a giant club, studded with iron spikes and nails. Several chains and manacles hung from his belt.

"Goblin!" Callan shouted, springing from his chair, his sword in hand.

"Stay your hand, human!" the giant jabbed a finger at the guard, who wisely stood still. Callan looked over at his captain, the Prosecutor, who motioned for him to put his sword down and retake his seat. Pulling himself up straight and thrusting his chest out, his hands upon his belt buckle, Prosecutor Smit waited as the orc closed the door against the storm and stepped forward. As tall as Smit was, his eyes were only level with the orc's chest.

"What brings you to human lands, orc?"

"In my clan, I am known as Orban Whitehair. What do they call you, human?" He glared downwards at Smit, his nostrils flaring as he sniffed the air.

"I asked, what brings you here?" Smit's eyes narrowed. Sondar could sense the unease not only between the two, but all within the room. Hands moved imperceptibly towards weapons; muscles tensed under armour. She glanced from Smit to Orban and back again.

"I seek a demon, a demon that has terrorised my people and the trail has led me here."

"Like us." Jontie piped up from his seat, then looked at Sondar. "Or most of us."

"You seek the demon known as Tor Baek as well?" asked Orban, glancing over towards the young man.

"A demon? That aptly describes the one I chase."

"But not all of us. We chase a murderer, and the acolyte here chases a beast." Prosecutor Smit raised a hand to quieten Jontie.

"And I pursue a monster, a beast at best." The wizard's apprentice said.

The orc threw his head back and gave a booming laugh, a laugh that echoed about the room. His fist thumped down upon the bar with a crash.

"It is Tor Baek! You all pursue Tor Baek!" The orc paused, looking at their incredulous and puzzled faces. He continued. "Tor Baek is a changeling, a shapeshifter. And he is here."

"Here?" asked Sondar. "You tracked it here?"

"Yes. I can smell him. His stench permeates the very air here."

"Here?" Jontie repeated Sondar's question.

"Yes, in this very room. The stench is strong." As if to accentuate his words he sniffed the air.

"I hope you are not implying that I am this beast you seek?"

Smit's voice remained calm, yet his hand moved towards the hilt of his sword.

"Yes, human. You or anyone else here. Or..."

The building plunged into darkness; every lamp being extinguished simultaneously. The hearth, likewise; the coals turning black, the embers fading and disappearing as if they never existed. Something thudded against the table that Sondar sat at, and she cursed as her flagon of ale sloshed over her arm. Smit cried out and there was a guttural expletive from Orban. Panicked shouts and cries came from the others, along with the sounds of steel being drawn from scabbards.

Throwing herself down to crouch, she flipped her table, hopefully in the right direction to form a barricade and drew her own daggers. To her left, Storn sat and whimpered in his stall, to her right and in front of her, came only the sounds of chaos. She thought she heard steel on steel, followed by a sharp intake of breath. Something splashed across her face as she crouched, causing bewilderment before the faint sickening metallic aroma told her it was blood. A footstep landed to her right and she lashed out instinctively, the dagger scraping against something hard.

Sondar jumped as the oil lamps flickered in life once more, the coals of the hearth behind her glowing orange and white once more. More tables and stools were overturned than standing correct. Storn still whimpered at the far end of his stall, his arms wrapped protectively around the books. She looked about; her own dagger had struck the upturned table and not an occupant of the inn. Peering over her makeshift barricade, she was pleased to see Jontie crouching by the bar. Smit and Callan stood back-to-back with swords drawn. Both panted heavily, yet their blades were clean. Garith, however, lay groaning on the floor, his hands raised to his head.

"What in all that is holy was that?" Jontie stood and tentatively moved towards the stricken man.

"No doubt the orc," sneered Smit, his eyes glancing across the room.

"I don't think it was him, Prosecutor," answered Sondar. She stood, pointing towards the figure of the orc, kneeling with his head bowed. A table had been torn asunder, and two heavy planks had been thrust through his chest. Blood and pieces of flesh adorned the jagged protruding ends that jutted from his back. A pool of scarlet seeped across the stone flags towards them.

"Only one of us with that power. Only one of us with the strength to do that to him." Callan muttered, staring at Garith as the holy man sat up.

"Didn't you hear him?" snapped Sondar.

"I judge only with my eyes, woman," growled Callan, taking a step towards Garith.

"Then I pity those accused in your land, Callan." Sondar stepped forward, the blade of her dagger pointing towards the floor.

"Callan!" Smit spoke, the authority clear in his voice. "Back up!" A raised hand blocked the guard from moving forward, and the Prosecutor turned to Sondar. She took the pause as an indication she should explain herself.

"Orban said the demon he chased, in fact the demon that you all chase, was a shapeshifter. And that means – "

"And that means that anyone of us could have done that." Jontie completed her sentence. "So, how do we deal with this?"

"There are six of us. We pair up," said the Prosecutor. "Three pairs, keeping an eye on each other."

"All well and good. Unless you are the one paired with the thing that just ripped an orc apart." Sondar dryly replied, shaking her head.

"I agree." Jontie turned back to the bar, banging his fist upon the top of it and shouted for the barman. "Barkeep! More ale! I think we should all sit here, facing each other until the thing makes it move. Then I'll get my chance to avenge my Elen and Jon."

Smit laughed.

"A chance to meet them again would be more likely!"

Jontie rounded on him, a hand outstretched to grab the arrogant officer of the law, his other fumbling for his sword at his side.

"What do you mean by that, you bastard?" he seethed, flecks of phlegm spitting from his mouth. His eyes blazed in anger. The path towards his taunter was abruptly ended as Smit's man, Callan, stepped across his path, delivering a stinging slap to his face. Sondar cried out as the young man fell to the floor.

"Do not!" Smit jabbed a finger in her direction, "you said it yourself. Anyone of us could be that thing. Worry about yourself, and how we find out who it is."

Garith righted himself, picking up a stool in the process and thumping himself down on it. He took a second to look over the room and take in the situation. His face blanched as he saw Orban.

"Blessed be the Child of Light." He raised the tips of his fingers to his temples as he mentioned his god. "What happened? I remember the darkness, then – "

"That is the very question that we ask ourselves." Smit intoned as he made his way towards the corpse of Orban.

"I must say," Garith pulled himself to his feet, aware after a few seconds that he wasn't going to get help. "I must say, I thought the way the inn was plunged into darkness, very sinister. Almost as if brought about by witchcraft." He stared at Storn as he sat down upon his stool.

"Or wizardry," spat Callan.

"It wasn't me," shrieked the older man, pushing himself further into the booth.

"That's strange, Garith. Someone may well have chosen the word; godlike." Sondar interrupted haughtily.

"The Child of Light does not – "

"Exactly! Flashing accusations around that are unfounded is not going to help."

"As annoying as she is, she is right. Work out a way to find out who this Tor Baek is." Smit added, not looking up from his inspection of the orc.

"Barkeep!" shouted Jontie. "Where *is* the man?"

"And his daughter," added Sondar, looking about.

Jontie leant over the bar, as if to get a better look.

"Strange." He called out. "There's a pile of dust here, right about where the barkeep was standing."

"One here too, by the hearth." Sondar replied. She didn't need to add that was where the young slip of a girl had been standing.

"Wait! There is something in the room behind!" Jontie vaulted the counter and drew his sword.

"Callan," Smit called. "Go with him!"

Sondar could sense the hesitation in the guard, not wanting to be away from his captain, nor possibly paired with a potential killer.

"Come on, Callan. I'll hold your hand." She grinned, thrusting the dagger back into her boot and drawing her short sword instead.

She made her way around the counter, nodding to the young Jontie. He gave a nervous grin, then gulped before shuffling forward. Sondar didn't check behind her to see if the guard was following, sensing his presence rather than seeing it.

The room behind the bar was a narrow storeroom. Barrels lined one wall, with old shelving on the other. Bottles filled the sagging shelves, the old wood threatening to crack under the weight. Apart from an old washbasin at the far end, above which was a small window that stood slightly ajar, there seemed little else in the room. A black shape flashed across the room, from behind the barrels towards the shelves. Callan lashed out with a sword, whilst Jontie leapt to one side, barrelling into Sondar, and knocking her to the floor. As the shape passed her, she made out what it was.

"It's a cat!"

It sprang to one shelve before vaulting onto the wash basin and onto the ledge of a small, open window. Callan lashed out again, the blade swinging harmlessly behind it.

"Stay your hand, man! What is wrong with you?"

"That's it! That's the shape changer!" Callan's eyes blazed red and wide. The cat turned almost to taunt him, before leaping to the highest shelf then squeezing itself through the open window and disappearing into the storm beyond.

"There's nothing else here." Jontie shook his head. "The noise I heard must have been that cat."

A shriek came from the main room, the sound carrying as if the air had been sliced with a knife. Callan turned and ran back the way they had come, followed by Sondar and Jontie. Prosecutor Smit stood ashen faced and silent. He stared at the crumpled figure in the brown robes. Sondar noticed a slight tremor in his left hand. Storn wailed like a banshee, his arms clasping his tomes once again across his chest. He sat with his back to the wall, his feet pulled up onto the bench.

Garith lay twisted and broken. Blood was already pooling about the body. Whatever had hit him had been immense. Even from where Sondar and the others stood, they could see the white of jagged bones piercing the umber robes. His features were destroyed, the once rosy face smashed into a scarlet hue.

"Prosecutor! What happened?" Callan called, leaping the bar to make for his captain. Smit could only stand frozen in horror. Sondar and Jontie nervously made their way from behind the bar and crossed to the wailing wizard.

"At least I know I'm not Tor Baek." Jontie muttered to no one in particular. For once, any joviality had left his voice. Sondar grabbed the wizard by his shoulders and shook him.

"Storn!"

Mercifully, at least to Sondar, the shrieking stopped, and the terrified eyes met hers.

"What did that to Garith?" She hissed through her teeth. The older man sobbed and pointed over her shoulder. Sondar followed his arm, and was surprised to see it point, not at Smit, but at the ceiling above Garith's body. At that point, the high ceiling stood two men's height above the floor, but all Sondar could focus on was the smear of crimson over the wooden planks. Whatever had killed the acolyte had picked him up and thrown him against the ceiling, smashing his huge body as easily as a thrush smashed a snail's shell.

Her muddled mind tried to calculate the strength needed to do that. Strength like that necessary to crack an oaken table apart and ram the pieces through the chest of an orc, she thought. It had to be either Smit or Storn, yet their reaction showed it wasn't. The arrogant Prosecutor hadn't spoken yet, and she wasn't sure whether he was catatonic with shock.

What her mind was telling her was unbelievable. Nothing she knew of had that sort of strength, yet the evidence stood before her, unless... Her mind raced, covering the other possibility that had come to her. Yet, recent events caused her not to cry out. Orban had been close to making a revelation, and then Tor Baek had killed him. She must not give the shape changer cause to strike again. Her hand clasped against the arm of Storn, and she could feel him tremble in fear.

"Storn, I need your help. You need to breathe slowly and surely." She smiled as he looked upon her and he seemed reassured. A brief nod was all that was needed.

"Come with me. We are going to walk across to where Prosecutor Smit is standing." She pulled him to his feet and half dragged; half propelled him towards the Prosecutor. "You too, Jontie."

Her free hand sought her belt, grasping a flask suspended from a laced tie. Jontie caught the movement with a sideways glance, and he watched as she removed the stopper. An almost imperceptible nod passed between them, and she was glad to see the young widower do the same. She whispered as they neared the two guardsmen.

"Storn, cast *Fieros!*" As she spoke, she tipped the flask upside down, pouring the contents onto the tables and stools that she passed. Jontie did the same, the pungent smell of the flammable lamp oil assailing their nostrils. Storn stared at her, his expression blank.

"Storn!" She shouted. He raised his fingers and clicked. A flame flickered into life and Sondar brought the flask up to it, dangling the lacing that had become soaked with oil onto its tip. The flame seemed to leap from the fingers of Storn to the lace, then roared upwards and engulfed the flask. She held it out to Jontie who lit his flask in similar fashion, then she hurled it at the nearest table.

As the tables and stools caught alight, the inn screamed in pain. A shriek that both rumbled and howled through the whole building. The walls and ceiling twisted in agony, deforming to punch out and strike the fires, trying to extinguish them. It only served to spread the flame further, within seconds the walls and ceiling were burning, black smoke rising towards the ceiling. Sondar coughed, the air acrid.

"What in Hell's name is happening?" Smit screamed as he pulled Callan out of the way of a man-sized fist that shot out from the wall.

"The inn is Tor Baek!"

"That means..." started Storn as realisation hit him.

"Yes, we're inside the demon!" Smit finished.

They ran for the doorway, dragging and pushing each other

along, desperate to escape the bowels of the demon. The scream continued, now not just a howl of pain as the demon's insides burnt, but a bellow of indignancy as its prey sought to escape. The floor of the Inn rippled, throwing them to the ground. Jontie crumpled against the wall, dazed. Smit and Callan pulled themselves up and smashed themselves against the door. It held up under their onslaught.

Sondar scrambled to Jontie's side, heaving the young man to his feet, placing an arm over her shoulder.

"Come on, Jontie." She didn't need to press the danger they were in. Storn shouted to the guardsmen to stand back, raising his arms, then propelling his hands towards the doorway, his lips muttering arcane words. A hurricane of air rushed past Smit, smashing the doorway to smithereens. Callan grabbed him and shoved him through the opening as blood dripped from the open wound in the demon's side.

"Hurry!" he urged, pulling the wizard towards him, whilst beckoning Sondar onwards. He never saw it, the beam punching him from behind, striking his head. He was dead before he hit the floor. Storn staggered past him, collapsing through the opening, the cold wet grass a blessing.

Sondar felt Jontie waken, the young man finding the energy and wherewithal to move. The shrieking was deafening now but Sondar tried to push it from her mind. The hole in front of them was still several strides away, yet Tor Baek was trying to heal himself. The wound was starting to close and the floor they staggered upon was slick with blood.

"Go!" Jontie called, blood frothing from his mouth as he spat the word out.

"No!" Sondar pulled him along as she reached out for the gap. Smit stood on the far side; his hand held out towards her.

"Take her, Smit!" Jontie wrenched himself free from her grasp, then shoved her as hard as he could. She fell into the wound, the walls now closing in on her, gripping her waist. She felt Smith grab her hands and heave. Tor Baek's wound squeezed her, helping to push her out, a macabre birthing in the wet of the storm.

Sprawling on the floor, she turned to see the wound close fully. The inn morphed into a roaring beast that threw itself up on two legs, the shrieking and howling no quieter now they were outside. As the legs came down, the demon morphed again, forming a huge chest, then back to a distorted version of the inn.

Storn raised his hands to chest height. The words he spoke disappeared into the storm, but Sondar watched as a ball of fire grew between them. Slowly he twisted and turned his hands, making them wider as the fireball grew.

"Wait! Jontie is still inside!" She called out, hands reaching for the wizard, as she scrambled to her feet. Smit grabbed her, pulling her back down to the sodden grass.

"There's nothing we can do for him now."

Her heart sank as she knew he was right. Jontie had gone to meet his wife and child. The inn shook in front of her, then twisted into an abomination. A lumbering humanoid beast with broad shoulders covered in scales and horns. It roared, his head thrown back, the cold rain striking its hideous features. This must be Tor Baek in his true form, she thought.

Storn shouted as he released the fireball, which hit Tor Baek in the chest. The arcane fire exploded, showering the area with flames which took hold even though the grass was wet. Tor Baek fell to his knees, the whole of his body engulfed. His fingers clawed at its throat and face, the flames stripping his airways from oxygen.

A guttural sound emanated from the ruined lungs and throat, and Tor Baek toppled onto his face, finally still. Sondar, Storn and Smit stared as the flames continued to burn, consuming the demon.

Smit placed his hand on Sondar's shoulder.

"Come, Sondar. He is at last at rest."

She looked up, the flames were dying now. The rain sizzled against the burnt body. She nodded, knowing it was over. The rain felt soothing on her face as it matted her hair.

"I am glad that you found your way to us, Sondar K'dar. Without you, we would still... it doesn't bear thinking about." Smit spoke, his hand still on her shoulder.

"As I said, Prosecutor Smit, I was just passing through." She looked up into the cloudy night sky and through a patch in the clouds, she saw three stars forming a perfect triangle. Smiling, she knew that Jontie had found his Elen and Jon.

The Journal of Abelard C. Grey.

Abelard C Grey, once of Her Britannic Majesty's Airship Corp, as we find him is in the employ of the Privateer Captain Hariman. A hero in a time that never was, in a world of steampunk technology. A world abounds with airships, mechanized horses pulling hansom cabs, submarines and advanced weapons. A globe that is still spanned by the British Empire, the 'Empire upon which the sun never sets', yet one that is populated by demons and wizards, gods and undead, fantastical creatures of all sizes, all hidden beneath a layer of crime and poverty, and political machinations of empires. Terrors that the ordinary population are, on the whole, blissfully unaware.

Abelard, and Boo – who we meet in The Isle of Kola T'ui, continue to push the boundaries within this steampunk world, just as the two of them push my imagination deep into the weird and wackiness that is the Steampunk/Gaslamp genre.

6

The Isle of Kola T'ui

This is the journal of Abelard C. Grey, born and raised in the village of Maulden in the year 1842 and formerly, a crewman in Her Britannic Majesty's Airship Corps. Whilst the tales told within this journal seem somewhat fanciful and from the realms of fantasy, they are – and I humbly swear upon my mother's life – that they are true. If anything, as I am writing these some years after the events occurred, my memories of them may have dulled overtime and reality was even more bizarre than my recollections. I start with a tale that concerns the beginning of my time as, though I should say career, rather than time, as I have made a tidy sum of the occupation, an adventurer.

Part, the first.
In which a secret cargo is loaded, and a plan (of some sorts) is hatched. An angel is discovered, along with a host of demons.

It was the summer of 1862. I was in my twentieth year and was no longer taking the Queen's Shilling, having left the employ of Her Majesty some months earlier. I was now serving under a Privateer, a Captain Edward Harriman on the air-brig Hyperion.

Having spent a few years in the HBMAC on the modern airships such as HMA Dreadnaught and HMA Furious, the Hyperion was a hybrid of technologies, both of yesteryear and the present. Built originally as a seagoing brig of the HMS Cruizer class, she had found herself obsolete before her time with the advent of airpower. As the navies of the world had sought to unburden themselves from the ties of nautical only ships, Hyperion and her sisters and cousins found themselves facing the breakers' yards. A lifeline was thrown to them due to the end of the War in the Crimea. When hostilities had ceased, sailors and airmen alike were decommissioned, and used their compensatory payments to buy these once majestic denizens of the sea. Some returned to the waves, their new owners unwilling to take to the skies. Many were converted to airships, and Hyperion was one of these.

Where acres of sail once hung was now home to a semi rigid lighter-than-air balloon, in the style of those produced by Professor von Zeppelin, a cylindrical gasbag that tapered to points at the bow and stern. Four tail fins projected from the stern of the gasbag like points of a compass. Slung below the greying fabric of the Zeppelin was a suspended walkway consisting of steel grill flooring that circumnavigated the outline of the main deck below. Where once sailors on board the deck below were open to the elements, both cruel and benevolent, now protection was offered in the form of glass walls fitted within immensely ornate steel frames that reached from gunwales to the zeppelin above. The main deck now had a climate akin to that of one of the greenhouses of the new industrialised farms that ran the breadth of the Old World. Indeed, Harriman's crew had taken advantage of this and several plants grew in the warm eco-system (as Mr. Darwin refers to it).

The Hyperion was powered by steam, a great furnace burnt away on the orlop deck below, with a small team of stokers continually shoveling coal into its fiery maw. The smokestack reached high, higher than the original main mast and penetrated the gasbag above, vomiting its foul, black smoke thankfully out of sight. This massive furnace powered a large propeller at the stern of Hyperion and helped propel the airship forward with the power of, or so I was told, several hundred horses. Two smaller steam engines were situated in small outriggers that hung in gondolas at the end of girders 10 yards long sited roughly amidships and slightly above the level of the main deck. These gondolas both had smaller propellers at their bows and a smokestack that angled slightly away from the ship in so much that the black smoke would drift harmlessly past Hyperion. Unfortunately, they failed miserably at this simple task.

Captain Edward Harriman was an unsavoury character, much more handsome in appearance than in attitude and personality. He could be cruel and heartless, but always wanted to do well for his crew. Ah, the crew. Yours truly aside, never has a more ragged bunch of individuals been seen. A complete hodge-podge of nationalities and languages. Only one step stood between the Hyperion and her crew and those that sailed under the mark of the Jolly Roger. Captain Harriman carried a letter of marque, a letter of authority issued by Her Britannic Majesty's Government to carry out acts of armed aggression against its enemies. Harriman was also happy to transgress from the rules should circumstance bless him and his crew with the opportunity to fill their pockets with extra gold. I have no doubt, if it wasn't for that short, handwritten letter, its script so beautifully written upon the heavy, buff paper, with its thick red wax seal, then Harriman and his crew would have danced the pirate jig from the yardarm of one of Her Majesty's Airships.

It was one of these such circumstances that this journal entry is about. The crew of the Hyperion had exhausted its supply of goodwill among the denizens of Port Stuart, a small town on the north coast of Australia. Harriman was looking to leave at dawn the next day with a view to patrol the islands in and around the Bismarck and Solomon Seas to the northeast. I was in the process of finishing repairs to the port outrigger when I heard the Bosun, Frank Bobo, and the captain in conversation on the main deck. Due to the heat, the glass panes that protected the deck were raised to allow airflow to the parched deck. I was sure that both officers were unaware that their voices were carrying to me in the gondola.

Their conversation seemed to be regarding a cargo, one that had yet to be loaded. As I explained earlier in the journal, I am writing these accounts several years after their occurrence, so my recollection as to the exacts words spoken that night may be amiss, but their sentiments and meaning remain the same.

'What says Iron Turner? Is it ready to move?' Harriman asked. Iron Turner was the name of a local sorter, a man who would arrange things for you - if someone wanted something found or sourced, a sorter would be the best place to start, especially if the route to such an item was on the wrong side of the law. He could arrange to grace palms with money (your money, obviously) to ensure that your desired outcome would occur. And if one should want something nefarious to happen to a business competitor, a rival suitor or a spurned lover, then a man such as Iron Turner would be your first port of call.

'He reckons midnight would be as good a time to pick it up as any, Cap'n.'

'And the cargo, he had it there? You saw it when you spoke.' Harriman asked the question of his bosun. The big man chuckled when he replied.

'Aye, Cap'n, and she is mighty fine.'

'My orders, Bobo, were to refer to her as "the cargo", and nothing else. Did I not make myself clear?'

'Of course, Cap'n. My mistake and it won't happen again.' Even his bosun seemed as scared of Harriman's temper.

'Well, we'll see about relaxing those terms when we've set sail.' The captain sneered. Nautical terms were still used by many airshipmen despite their ships never touching the waves.

'Now then,' he continued. 'Take five men ashore with you. Choose wisely from the Circle. I would say Martensen the Dane, Corben and Jones to be amongst them.' This piqued my interest as I had been aware for some time that certain members of the crew were part of a cabal, a cadre who obtained special privileges from Harriman. It may have only been being chosen for watch during better weather, or less labourious tasks whilst in dock, but there was a certain hierarchy within the crew. Not that it was written, nor spoken about, but to the inquisitive eye, it was as apparent as the almost imperceptible tip of a snowdrop breaking the frozen earth in January.

'Armed and ready for danger, Bobo. This cargo is the key to a treasure the size and value of which we can only dream of.' With those words, Harriman waved his Bosun away and stood staring from the deck, away to the northeast and to the open sea.

THE SIX MEN returned just after Four Bells in the Middle Watch. For those unlearned in naval terminology this would be 2.00am, an ungodly hour for all sane people. Between four of them, suspended from two poles held tight upon their shoulders, was what appeared to be a crate, obscured as it was by a piece of sail canvas. The Bosun walked behind, a blunderbuss clutched to his chest. Martensen, the huge Dane led, an imposing figure at the best of times, but even more so with a brace of pistols thrust through his belt and a huge boarding axe in his hands. Harriman was there to see their arrival.

I had maintained my position in the gondola, having completed my repairs some time earlier. My stomach rumbled ominously to remind me of the fact that I had missed evening supper due to my vigil. I was determined to see what Harriman's secret cargo was, and why knowledge of it was excluded from all but his inner cartel. As well as placing more of his trusted men on guard duty, the captain had also allowed an extra rum ration which, though not unheard of, was against his very nature.

From my vantage point I could gain little benefit in discerning the nature of the cargo, mainly due to the covering canvas. My fellow crew members seemed to be under no discomfort whilst bearing the load, even after the two miles from Iron Turner's manor, so the weight of the cargo and chest combined would be less than half a dozen hundredweight. The chest itself, from what I could discern from how the canvas hung, seemed to be about five-foot-long and possibly two foot wide and deep. I was reminded of the dimensions of a coffin, albeit slightly shorter.

Harriman directed the maneuvering of the cargo into his cabin. The crewmen left, the Dane clutching a bottle of rum in his oversized hands as they went, leaving the Captain and the Bosun alone. I decided I could discover no more tonight and silently made the crossing between the gondola and the main hull by way of the walkway on top of the covered coal conveyor. I returned to my hammock, loudly complaining of my need to visit the head due to the extra grog, and hopefully sounding as rumdum as I could.

. . .

I AWOKE next morning to the sensation that Hyperion was underway. Upon enquiring the time from my companion next to me I was pleased to find I had slept to the end of Morning Watch. I spent most of the working day at my station with my thoughts wandering to what was in that chest in Harriman's cabin.

Our course took us to the northeast, as was the original intention of the captain when we had arrived at Port Stuart. If we steered clear of the eastern most tip of Nueva Guinea, which by all accounts would be a blessing and a wise move as the ungodly heathens there were headhunters, then our next sight of land would be the archipelago known as the Solomon Islands. A collection of islands, isles, and atolls covering a vast area, the archipelago numbered a thousand or more islands. Many were uncharted and even more untrodden by civilised man.

As I worked, I listened to the rest of the crew, anxious to hear if any others suspected anything amiss. In particular, I paid attention to Harriman's circle. It was to my frustration that I heard not one word about the cargo, nor any contradiction to the original mission of patrolling the Solomon Islands and the Bismarck Sea. There was only one course of action left to me. I would have to spy within Captain Harriman's cabin.

During the evening meal I lit the touch paper on my plan. On a regular navy ship, either a traditional sea-going ship or an airship, the stokers would be a separate division, working their own watches with little interaction with the workload in other parts of the ships. Here on the Hyperion, with the slightly reduced and stretched crew of a privateer, there were no stokers. Each watch provided men to do the labourious task of shoveling the coal from the bunkers deep in the hull either into the main furnace which drove the main propellor, or onto the conveyors which transported the coal along the chutes to the outrigger engines. The task was backbreaking and seemingly Sisyphean. No matter how fast or hard one shoveled, the bunkers never seemed to empty.

As terrible a task as that was, and at the tropics the heat and climate made the task even more herculean. Stokers had been known to expire from exhaustion, dropping dead mid shovel. It was one of the most dangerous tasks in an airship, made even more horrifying when the ship was under attack. Despite the danger, it was not the most uncomfortable task on Hyperion. That position was the aft lookout.

The lookout positions are akin to the crow's nest of old but enclosed in a semi-rigid cupola on top of the outer envelope. The Hyperion has two of these positions; fore and aft. Due to the catenary curve of the gas bag, the fore station only gives a view of the course ahead and to either side. The aft station is the opposite, whereas it only gives a view of the course from whence Hyperion had travelled.

One would assume that a watch spent as a lookout would be an easy task, but then one would be mistaken. The cupolas were small and cramped, with not enough room to lay down straight. They were reached by a ladder that squeezed between two of the internal gas bags and were entered by way of a trapdoor. The aft station was above one of the hot air bags, (Hyperion being a composite machine, consisting of alternating hydrogen and hot air bags, held within the main envelope.) which made the station more bearable whilst within the polar circles, but unbearable whilst in the tropics. The only ventilation was in the form of two small windows that opened to either side, however the smoke from the smoke-stack often drifted across the cupola, which gave the unlucky incumbent a choice between choking on thick, black smoke or roasting in the insufferable heat.

It was at evening meal, when Bobo came to apportion out

the duties for the First Watch, which runs from 8.00pm to midnight, that my plan started to be put into action.

'Frenchie, take the fore station lookout, Collins aft station.' The small man groaned, his shoulders sinking, almost taking him to the deck. The Bosun ignored him and continued.

'Big John, Anders, and Grey. Stoking.'

I groaned, almost as loud as the diminutive Collins. Bobo looked at me, he had a habit of piercing your very soul with his glare.

'It's me back, sir. It's been aching for a good while. Stoking will do me in. Is there anything lighter.' Bobo was about to dress me down when Collins broke in.

'You can take my watch at aft, Grey. You're welcome to it!' I screwed my face up in disgust.

'You don't have to take it, Grey. Enjoy your shoveling.'

I threw my arms up and suddenly grimaced in what I hoped was a good impersonation of a man with back ache and reached quickly for the small of my back.

'I'll take your watch, Collins.' I looked across to the Bosun. 'If you have no objections, sir?' The big man grunted and turned away.

And so, I found myself crouched in the aft lookout station as the sun disappeared over the horizon, plunging the sky into darkness. With my heart in my mouth, I pushed open one of the small vents. For once the smoke drifted harmlessly away and I breathed in a mouthful of clean, fresh air. Steeling myself, I pushed first one arm, then my head through the opening. It was tight but I managed to squeeze through, holding precariously with one hand to one of the several heavy catenary ropes that helped secure the envelope. And then I slithered over the curve of the envelope, hand over hand on the rope, thankful that it was mostly dark so that I could not see the depths of the fall below me. As I slipped over the side of the world, I realised that this was the most insane and lunatic thing that I had attempted.

Thankfully the course of the Hyperion stayed true and the wind was only a light breeze. I made better progress when the rope finally came away from the side of the envelope and gas bags and I quickly made my way down until I stood on the rail that surrounded the poop deck. Underneath my feet was Captain Harriman's cabin. There was, perhaps four or five feet between the deck roof and the lowest point of the hydrogen and air-filled envelope. Because of this, I believe that I was possibly the first person to stand upon the poop deck for several years. And, having been present in the captain's cabin on but two occasions, I knew that the glass skylight was still present. I slithered on my belly like a serpent until I could peer through the glass into the cabin below.

Harriman sat at his desk, poring over charts with a goblet of red wine in his hand. He was stripped to his shirt and breeches and his long dark hair was pulled back and secured in a queue. I hardly dared breathe as my eyes roamed around the room. What I had done, leaving my station, was at best a flogging offence. Espying on the Captain, could in some courts, be tantamount to mutiny, which could be punished by hanging or walking the plank. The chest that had contained his cargo was uncovered, revealing its true form. It was built in the style of a cage, with a solid floor and steel barred walls and lid. The lid was open.

My heart skipped a beat as I saw the creature that had once been caged within. Seated upon a stool in front of the captain's desk was the most beautiful creature I had ever seen. And in that list, I include my very own Clara, waiting somewhere back in Bedfordshire. Whilst I remained true to Clara throughout my adventures, her true beauty came from inside, her softness, her willingness to please and help, and her naivety all combined with her feminine charms to make her Beauty personified. The siren who perched on the wooden stool inside the captain's cabin was something else.

It was as if Spring and Summer, along with Aphrodite and Gaia had breathed life into the Venus de Milo. Any man would have laid siege to the very walls of Troy itself to watch over her beauty. My words, as much as I can try, do not do justice to her. Should I write from now until the Day of Judgement, I could not fully describe her beauty.

Her form was elegant and full bodied, and her porcelain skin was laid bare for all to see. Upon her arms and back, and across her breasts were tattoos of a naval nature - pennants, anchors and the like along with skulls and hearts. Whilst most unfeminine in nature, they added a form of allurement to her charms. Her black hair flowed like satin across her shoulders and the contrast only made the milkiness of her skin even more white. She was chained from her ankle and her wrist to the cage. I watched for several minutes, mesmerised by the rise and fall of her breasts and desperately tried to think of my Clara instead.

Harriman placed his goblet down and stood. Removing any last vestiges of humanity from his soul, he then committed an act so atrocious that I cannot bring myself to divulge any further. Needless to say, that no woman should endure such distress, humiliation or pain such as the anonymous beauty did then. He left her sobbing, doubled up in pain and strode for the door, lacing his breeches as he walked.

I heard him call for Bobo, and the big man must have been standing nearby as he appeared quickly, as if conjured in some parlour trick. He held a small, red baize bag in his hand, the like of which needed no introduction to me, but to the naive prisoner unversed in the ways of the navy this should have held no suspicion. To my surprise, she recoiled in fear, still whimpering and crying. As a navy man for five years, I knew the 'Captain's daughter' well. A colloquial name for the cat'o'nine tails, a switch made up of nine knotted cords that could lay a man's back to the bone in several lashes. A man's back, or a woman's.

I watched as Bobo let the cat out of the bag as Harriman bent close to her ear and whispered. I could not make out what the captain had said but the woman shook her head vigorously, biting her lip. The Bosun pulled his arm back and flicked the cat against the bare back of the woman. A teaser at first, I thought, aware of what power the big man could put into his strikes. She didn't make a sound; I will give the siren that much. She did, however, bite into her lip. The scarlet hue of blood that seeped down her otherwise flawless chin seemed to excite Harriman no end. He turned to his desk and poured himself more wine, taking a deep sip before grabbing a chart. He held it out in front of his captive and shouted seven words that I heard with ease.

'Tell me where the island is sited!'

She shook her head again, her black hair matted to her face by sweat and tears. Bobo struck again, harder this time, knocking the breath from her. From that point, the intensity of the scene only accelerated. Harriman bounded around like a lunatic in bedlam, his shouting becoming louder and louder, his question repeated in so many forms. Bobo strikes accented by the crack of the cat on her back and her shrill shrieks and sobs. I could not watch and lay on the roof of the cabin, on my back staring up at the gas bag. Unfortunately, my mind was an avid a torturer as Harriman was, and I could not escape the vision of pain that my Beauty was in. There, I said it. My Beauty. For some reason, no doubt of chivalrous intent fashioned after some long-forgotten ancestor, I had adopted the responsibility of the siren as my own. I would be her saviour.

Then the cabin below went quiet. I rolled over and peered through the glass again. My Beauty sagged on the stool, one hand clutching a quill. Harriman held the chart out directly under my vantage point and I could see the addition of a ragged cross on one of the islands, marked in black ink. Bobo pushed his big hand into the matted hair of the woman and pulled her head up sharply. It was then that our eyes met. She could see the shame, disgust and hurt in mine, yet where I expected to see the same in hers, I did not. Her eyes were big, the colour of chestnuts and they shone, they were not dull with humiliation or pain but shone brightly with what I could only describe as one thought.

I rolled away, puzzled. Below I could hear Harriman say to Bobo to assemble the Circle, that they could all join in the merriment for the rest of the night. I retched, hoping to God on high that the sound would not carry. The ship's bell rung out and I realized that I would only have thirty minutes to return to my station before my replacement came. I made the perilous ascent without mishap and squeezed back into the cupola. Barely minutes later, Ali, the Muhammedan was knocking gently on the cupola trapdoor. I muttered incoherently that there was nothing to report and hurriedly made my way down the ladder, climbing into my hammock as fast as I could.

Barley an hour later, I awoke. My sleep broken by nightmares; visions of the crime committed by Zeus against Leda that were no doubt being carried out in Harriman's cabin like some obscene, devilish mummer play. I felt I needed to change my historical comparison because if the woman was Leda, that elevated Harriman to the position of Zeus, and although he was master and commander of the Hyperion, there was nothing godlike about his nature. My mind also wandered to the look that I had seen in the woman's eyes. It wasn't pain or humiliation, but victory. I therefore attributed the persona of Boudicca to her, the vengeful Iceni Queen.

Confused, but with anger rising at her mistreatment and also my failure to protect my charge, I swung from my hammock. I grabbed my pistol, making sure that the three round clip was fitted and the safety switch in the off position. My boots were already on, and I strode purposefully out of the cabin.

My luck was in as I crept across the deserted deck. I slowly opened the captain's cabin door and stepped in. Harriman lay asleep on his bunk, expended. The cabin was empty apart from Boudicca, as she was now known to me. She lay in her cage, the lid closed. She seemed asleep but as I glided to her side, her eyes opened. The look of victory still blazed but there was also something else. Hope. But I also saw the reflection in her dark pits of movement behind me, which possibly saved my life. I turned and started to stand, the Bosun's blow landing on my shoulders instead of my head. He had been sitting behind the cabin door on guard. Even though the severity of the blow was mitigated by my sudden movement, I still was sent reeling to the floor. My pistol was sent flying from my grasp and I floundered on my back like a fish out of water.

Harriman bounded to his feet, fully alert at the first sound of trouble. He picked my pistol from the floor and stood between me and the cage.

'What do we have here, Bobo?'

'Looks like a mutineer, Capt'n.' the big Bosun growled.

'It certainly does so, come to kill the captain and have a bit of fun with the treasure, eh?' he waved the pistol in the direction of Boudicca in the cage. My head swam as I answered.

'I came to rescue her.' I muttered.

'Oh, very noble and gentlemanly of you, Grey. And where were you going to rescue her to?' Harriman gloated; his words sickly sweet. 'If you had remembered, we are at five hundred feet above the Pacific Ocean. Land isn't in sight even from this altitude. Where would you go?'

I cursed, at my own fallacy. I had been driven to an insane act for want of acting correctly. Now, I would be paying for that failing with my life.

'What is the punishment for mutiny, Mr Bobo?' The Bosun folded his arms across his barrel chest and smiled.

'A flogging, a dozen lashes from each mate, then keel-hauling or the plank. Me personally, I prefer to watch them dance alongside the hull. Makes for a great spectacle.' Keelhauling on an airship was similar to that of a sea-going ship, the prisoner bound and then dragged along the underneath of the hull by way of ropes and pulleys. The rough facing of the wooden hull would have the same effect of barnacles and molluscs that were common to the hulls of sea ships, cutting the unfortunate victim to pieces. Any way to go and meet the Maker is unpleasant, but some are more unpleasant than others.

My left hand dived to my boot, grabbing my knife. I fancied a quick bullet rather than the slow protracted death that fate seemed to have written for me. Harriman fired, the sound echoing about the closed cabin, and the closeness sending a ringing to my ears. Boudicca screamed, but it was my body that exploded into pain. A thousand needles of fire seemed to lunge up my left arm. The knife was nowhere to be seen, along with hand. Fingers and all were blown to smithereens, and blood coursed from my shattered wrist. I reached across and gripped it, frantically trying to stem the flow.

'Keelhauling it will be then,' Harriman smiled. 'But not tonight. You see, Grey, this woman here is not the innocent beauty that you think she is, she's a witch, a hag and a siren. The Great Harlot from Revelations. She is all that and more. You may think, in your addled brain, that she is a jewel in the crown of this desperate existence that we call life, but she isn't. She is the map to *the* treasure. The mystical isle of Kola T'ui, where Zheng Jing, the pirate Prince of Yanping reputedly harboured one season. His treasure fleet was five merchantmen, five ships full of the treasures of the East. This harlot, is one of the keepers of the hoard, sworn to keep its secrets. Bobo can be quite persuasive though. She gave up the longitude and latitude last night. and we will make landfall on Kola T'ui tomorrow at noon. You will see the share of the treasure that you have just given up before I execute you. And after that, when we are next back home, I'll deliver the news of your demise to your good wife myself.'

He spat at me, then stood. By now two more crewmen had come running at the sound of the discharge. He bade them bind my arm and stop the bleed. As they did, I looked across to Boudicca, whose face alternated to and from my darling Clara's. In her dark brown eyes, I saw despair for the first time and her lips moved, yet I could not make out the words. In my pain wracked mind, I hoped that they thanked or forgave me, and I hoped that Clara would also forgive the consequences of my actions. Then the world went black.

Part, the second.
Ashore on the Isle. Giants amongst us, and the treasure of Zheng Jing. A defendant once again, with punishments to fit the crime.

I AWOKE the next day at noon. I say awoke, I had apparently been in and out of consciousness since the moment my hand had been blown away, but I remembered nothing of it. Several members of the crew, especially those from Africa, thought I was possessed and had pleaded with Harriman for me to be shot and cleansed. Intent on watching me suffer, and dance a jig with the ship's hull later, he declined. I was more conscious and coherent now, my wound having been crudely cauterised, which seemed to have killed the nerves, either that or one of my more sympathetic crew mates had injected me with morphine. It had also been badly bandaged, leaving me with what looked like a discoloured club for a hand.

The Hyperion was now landed upon the beach, which I took to be Kola T'ui. I was unceremoniously pulled to my feet and a rope was tied round my neck, not so tight as to impede breathing but tight enough to be uncomfortable. The other end was attached to Martensen's wrist and he took great delight in warning me to keep up when we set off. Boudicca appeared next to me, wearing only the ugly welts of her torture from the night before. Strangely enough, even though the flogging had occurred less than twelve hours before, the wounds were already healing faster than I thought possible. Her hands were bound, the end of that rope also attached to Martensen.

Harriman had ordered the disembarkation of a large landing party. Two thirds of Hyperion's crew mingled on the beach; forty men armed to the teeth. The man himself appeared, ready to lead. He had shunned his heavy coat and captain's jacket and stood only in breeches and a white silk shirt. He did carry his customary cutlass and a brace of pistols were thrust into his belt. The crew seemed in high spirits, so had obviously been told of Zheng Jing's treasure.

The captain ordered them to move off and we walked in double file, entering the jungle undergrowth. Even though the foliage was fairly dense, we kept a fast pace. Both myself and Boudicca stumbled often, only to be pulled to our feet by the immense frame of the Dane. The second time she fell, I reached out to steady or catch her, and for the first time I touched her. Martensen laughed.

'That is good, Grey. Why don't you give your girlfriend a hand? A hand?' This amused him even more and he chuckled to himself for several minutes.

I will not bore the reader with too much description of the jungle, suffice to say that certain words spring to mind; vines, palms, tangled roots and movement everywhere. What I will say though, there was an atmosphere about the place. A sense of foreboding dread that started to weigh almost as much as the heat and humidity. It seemed as if the island was warning us to leave and never return. I swore to Almighty God that if I lived, I would heed the notice. I looked about; all the crew were feeling the same as myself. The good cheer had disappeared, replaced with furtive glances into the jungle and over each shoulder. Many made the sign of the cross as they walked and muttered under their breath. Only two of the group seemed not to notice or care. Boudicca and Harriman.

It was after an hour of walking that we came across what can only be described as the temples. Vast buildings made of stone situated within a clearing. Straight avenues were marked out between them and the paths seemed well trodden and devoid of weeds or vegetation. The buildings themselves were akin to the ziggurats and temples that one might stumble across in the Americas and the Amazon. I had spent several months there whilst in the employ of Her Majesty, so am well versed in the architecture.

We started to make our way tentatively down the main avenue, between several of the smaller buildings. It was then a great hullaballoo started. It appeared that some of the men in the right-hand file had seen two women, similar in appearance and stature to Boudicca. They had broken rank and chased them into the buildings, shouting and cheering as was the way with men when they are in a state of pillage. They pulled the women back to the main body, which only encouraged more of the men to enter and investigate the nearest buildings.

Then they appeared. A sight to behold but, from the effect that they had on the other crew, the bizarreness of the situation was not a result of my morphine or feverish state. They were men, of that I have no doubt. But they towered over even Bobo or Martensen in height and stature. From the distance that I saw them from, I estimated their height to be ten feet or more.

Their skin had a green tinge to it, but if it wasn't for that, one would say they were the perfect specimen of Man, broad shouldered and muscular. They wore breechcloths which were decorated in bright colours on the panel that hung in front, but wore little else, except for a metal head band that circled their foreheads, and golden gauntlets that made their already large fingers appear bigger. Appearing one either side and in front, they made their way towards us.

'I have come for the treasure of Zheng Jing! I intend to take it with or without bloodshed!' shouted Harriman. He seemed surprised at their appearance but not perturbed. They made no answer but closed the distance to a dozen yards.

One of the crewmen, I remember not which one, raised his rifle and fired. The bullet hit one of them in the shoulder and he stepped back, flinching. We all looked as a small circle appeared and dark red blood seeped out. This was a modern rifle that should have had the stopping power to put a wild horse straight down. He stared at the wound, then turned back to face his assailant. As the crewman fumbled with his rifle to draw the bolt back to fire again, the giants clenched their fists and the gloves changed form. From the left-hand glove appeared a disc of yellow light, opaque enough to see through, that seemed to solidify at the edge. From the right glove, a pistol shape appeared, golden as the glove. The shot giant raised his right hand and a yellow bolt flew from the gun into the crewman, blasting a hole right through his chest.

The crew of Hyperion started to fire, however the discs of light that the giants carried seemed to be some sort of shields. I had no idea at the time whether this was science or magic. Bullets struck the shields and were immediately rendered useless, as if they had been fired at a sheet of five-inch steel. Even though the Hyperion outnumbered the giants four to one, they were severely outgunned. Soon half the Hyperions were down, dead of injured and only two of the giants were incapacitated, their shields not covering the whole of the body.

Harriman, seeing his dreams turn to nightmares grabbed one of the women that had been apprehended by the crew. Holding her in front of him as a shield, he held his pistol to her head.

'Stop!' he screamed. The skirmish had reached a natural lull, so his voice was heard above the sounds of gunfire and the sobs of the wounded. 'Stop! Or she gets it. We'll take the treasure and when we are back on our ship, we'll let them go.' The largest giant stopped to consider. Seeing that, several more of the airmen grabbed the women to use as shields. Martensen pulled on Boudicca's tether, with the intent on hiding his large frame behind her. For the most part of the battle, Boudicca and I had cowered on the floor. Now I staggered to my feet and, as the Dane turned slightly from me, I landed a kick straight to the side of his knee, sending him to the floor with a scream of pain, almost as loud as the crack of bone that had shattered under my kick. I positioned myself in front of Boudicca, willing to shield her with my own body. He raised himself up on his good knee and slowly raised his pistol at us.

A shot rang out and he collapsed. I, or Boudicca, had been saved by one of the giants. The largest giant now stepped forward to Harriman and spoke in a slightly stilted accent, but in very good English.

'Let her go, and you will live.' He held out his hand, the pistol disappearing from view as quickly as it had appeared. Harriman shook. Not just his arm but his whole body. He seemed to be fighting some urge projected by the now calm voice of the giant. He snarled, his true form starting to overcome the power of the giant. Spittle flew from his mouth as he turned red, finally screaming in a demonic voice.

'Be damned with you!' and he fired. The shot rang out, echoing around the clearing. The woman sagged and

Harriman allowed her to fall. The giant closed the distance between them in an instant and struck the captain an almighty blow about the head, knocking him unconscious. Seeing this, the rest of the crew threw down their arms and surrendered.

Boudicca shrugged herself free from her bonds and walked to the tallest of the green men. He smiled and wrapped her in a big hug. She only came up to his abdomen, and she rubbed her face over the muscular body and breathed in his scent. They talked briefly in a language that I didn't understand, Boudicca craning her neck upwards to gaze into his eyes as they talked. It was more than evident that they knew each other, possibly intimately.

Finally, the giant nodded to his men and they prodded the remaining Hyperions, myself included towards the largest of the temples. One of the giants picked Harriman up as if he was a sack of wheat, throwing the inert body over his shoulder. As I marched off with the rest of the crew, I looked behind me and was distressed to see the naked women dispatching my injured crewmates with as little concern as a farmer's wife wringing a hen's neck. The temple that we were led towards had several wide steps leading up to the entrance. The top step formed a large platform edged by several stone columns that held aloft the roof.

Boudicca stood on this step next to the giant. As each man reached the top step, she either nodded or shook her head. Those she nodded to were thrust into the temple, the others were pushed to one side and forced to their knees, looking back down the avenue to the scene of the massacre. About halfway through the crewmen I noticed a pattern, those who were entering the temple were Harriman's circle. Bobo, Corben and Jones entered along with several others. The giant carrying Harriman walked straight through and deposited him on the floor. When I reached the top step, Boudicca took hold of the rope that was still knotted about my neck and guided me to her side. She neither nodded or shook her head and the giant looked at her with a slight look of puzzlement.

One of the giants, one who was almost as tall as the leader, with a shock of white hair atop his head made his way along the line of kneeling men. He inspected each one, choosing some to go inside the temple until only a handful were left. He then nodded to those that guarded them and they were led away.

'What is to become of them?' I asked.

Boudicca only shook her head and then guided me inside.

The interior of the temple was rudimentary and sparse. A huge chair was set at one end which the leader of the giants sat upon as he surveyed the prisoners. They had all been stripped and now knelt on the stone floor, ropes tied about each wrist which were tied to iron rings in the floor, holding their arms out to the side. Harriman was awake, and he returned the giant's stare. The others knelt with their heads bowed. Boudicca led me to the front and indicated that I knelt next to Harriman. She tied the end of the rope to the ring, leaving my arms free.

I looked about the room. The women had now returned and stood with their men, the giants. They clasped themselves to their legs and waists, rubbing their hands over the huge bodies in brazen, wanton displays of affection. It was obvious that the women, and Boudicca, despite their size, were consorts of the giants. My mind spun at the consequences of this along with other questions that I really didn't want to know the answers to. My stomach heaved and I vomited my last meal on the floor in front of me.

'Now this is a turn up for the books, Grey.' Harriman sneered next to me.

'Yes, it is. It does look like that we are both to meet our Maker today.'

'The only question is, which of us is to be the first? I wonder if I will get the opportunity to witness your exit.'

'You really are a sick individual, Harriman.' I avoided the use of his rank, having decided long ago that he was unfit to captain me.

'Silence!' The giant clapped his hands. He then addressed Boudicca.

'Gwa Gia. You have done well in your mission, going out into the wide world and bringing these humans to us in order to swell our ranks. Their airship has been captured and even now, the remainder of the crew have been taken to the farm. I am disappointed though, that you have refused to classify this one with its eventual fate. Why?' As he spoke, he pointed at me.

Boudicca or Gwa Gia as the giant had called her, moved to stand near me. As she walked, I kept my eyes on her face, trying to fathom her out. Now I was aware of that look in her eye, that glint of victory that I had seen from my vantage point above Harriman's cabin.

'Because this one, Kola Nor, this Grey, stayed true to his woman, the love of his life that dwells the other side of the world. It would have been easy for him to descend into the depths of depravity that these animals did, but he did not. Furthermore, he endeavoured to save me and forfeited his life when he failed. I know the danger that he faced as he made the decision to stand against his commander.'

'You say he forfeited his life, yet he kneels before me now. Is he not alive?' The court against me proceeded, the second one that had presided over my fate in the last twenty-four hours. Not many men can say that.

'He is a dead man walking. That beast would have him keel-hauled for daring to attempt my rescue, for standing up for my virtue.' At the mention of the fate that awaited me, the women in the temple murmured between them.

'Yet he still breathes.' My judge seemed to not be understanding.

'Your defence seems to be losing, Grey.' Harriman sneered. My heart leapt into my mouth, and my head swam. My hand, or lack of hand thereof, had started to ache again, whatever pain relief now subsiding.

'If I may speak?' I waited for an acknowledgement, but none was forthcoming, so I proceeded. 'Gwa Gia is correct. I did attempt to rescue her, but not before she had endured terrible torture, which was carried out almost as soon as I was aware of her existence. Maybe you are right, maybe I should have stepped up earlier.'

Harriman laughed.

'Maybe you should stay with your original defence lawyer.' he commented snidely.

I ignored him and continued.

'But if I had, I fear that we would not be here now.'

'But when you did, it was too late, and you failed in your undertaking.' It wasn't a barbed comment, but a factual statement from the giant, Kola Nor.

'And that rankles me. I not only signed my own death warrant, but placed the love of my life, my wife Clara, in danger.' I held my shattered hand aloft. 'This wound stopped me from furthering my plan.'

Kola Nor nodded to one of his companions who then made his way to me. Taking my arm in his giant hands, he stripped away the bandages leaving the ugly wound open to see. And smell. I was sure at that point, that if Kola Nor didn't execute me, or if Harriman couldn't escape to carry out his plan, that I would be dead of infection in a few hours. As I looked down at the burnt wound, something struck me. Something that had been said moments before.

'Wait! Kola Nor, am I to assume that Gwa Gia went on her own volition, into the world to find us, directly or indirectly?'

'I have already said that it was her mission. For years we have taken our workforce and our companions,' as he mentioned these he indicated with a wave of his hand to the general outside and then to the women who still held themselves to the giants, 'from those that landed or were shipwrecked on our island. Those that came to find the treasure of Zheng Jing. But over time, Zheng Jing has become forgotten and the tide of seekers have diminished. We decided to spread the word of Kola T'ui far and wide, to bring seekers once again to our shores. And for that task, I chose my most trusted wife, Gwa Gia. She has, after all, been with me the longest. Gwa Gia has played her part in enticing, seducing and tricking many of your sort to this Isle.'

At his words, I was beside myself with rage. I stood as tall as I could, which was difficult being tethered to the floor by way of a noose. I pointed angrily at Kola Nor.

'You dare to accuse me of failing to save a woman in the hands of animals, when it was you who put her there? How did you think she would be treated out there in the flea pits of the edges of the Empire, where life is cheap and often too short? You speak of the treasure of Zheng Jing, but gold and gems pale before beauty such as hers. If you had sent an old crone out to the world to tell of Kola T'ui, then animals such as Harriman would still have come, desperate for the trappings of wealth and fortune. Yet you sent your greatest treasure, Gwa Gia, your wife?'

'Very good, Grey. Interesting defence, accusing the judge of insanity.' Harriman again from beside me.

Kola Nor sat forward, his head resting on his chin. He stared straight at me, then across to Boudicca as a sense of realization washed over him.

'True, my actions did put you at risk.' He stood and stepped down to where Boudicca stood. 'What can I do to put this right?'

'I wish to leave, Kola Nor. I have been here longer than any other consort, more years than the years I spent in the wide world. I need to return. What little I saw of this new world whilst I carried out my task, whether it was good or evil, intrigued me to want to see more.' Kola Nor slowly nodded and held out his hand to Gwa Gia, who then continued.

'And I want to take this one with me.' she indicated me and for the first time, smiled at me. I smiled back and lifted my hand in front of me.

'I fear it will be only for a short time.'

'Can you do something, husband?'

Kola Nor nodded again to the companion who had removed my bandage. He left for a few minutes and returned, carrying a small plate. On it was a small pot containing a thick, sweet-smelling poultice and a lozenge.

'Take the lozenge, it will help with the pain.' Gwa Gia spoke. I hesitantly picked it up and popped it into my mouth. After all, if I was to be killed, they could have already done so. It tasted of clementines and vinegar, slightly acidic though not altogether unpleasant.

The giant took my arm again. This time he flexed his glove and a spear of yellow light appeared, rather than a disc. It was the length of a kitchen knife and with it he proceeded to carve quickly and extremely neatly. I stared in amazement as the light pierced my arm, cutting and cauterising at the same time. Even more to my amazement, I felt no pain at all. It was as if I was watching the procedure carried out on someone else. Finally, he spread the gloop of the poultice over it.

Kola Nor clapped his hand and spoke loudly, his voice carrying far beyond the temple. It was a simple verdict upon Harriman and the crew.

'The rest of you are guilty. Prepare for your punishment.' Harriman spat at the green giant.

'Damned be you and your harlots!'

The women removed themselves to the rear of the temple, where a stone altar held various pieces of equipment. I could not see exactly what from where I stood. Gwa Gia, Boudicca had produced a simple knife from somewhere and cut the rope from around my neck.

'Come, Grey. We should leave now.' She seemed agitated.

'No!' Kola Nor bellowed. Everyone stopped and Boudicca looked at him, her face pleading with him.

'He can't see this. Please Kola Nor, for me!'

'No, it will be my condition of his leaving here. After this, you can leave. I'll trade the Hyperion for a small airship that will only require a small crew to operate.' He looked at me and commanded me to stand with him as he returned to his seat. Boudicca burst into tears and ran from the temple. I looked confused and distraught. I should be comforting someone who had just pleaded for my life and was now in distress, yet I was bidden to stay.

'Leave her for now. You need to watch this. This will be your fate should you return to Kola T'ui unbidden. If I have need of you or Gwa Gia, you will come under truce, you have my word on that.' It was all I could do to nod in acknowledgement.

The women returned, some holding giant ivory horns and others with jugs. They stood in front of Jones first, who from my time on the Hyperion, had proven himself to be a violent sadist. I almost felt sorry for the man. He still knelt, the ropes holding his arms outstretched. His short brown hair was dank and thinning, despite his youngish age. I was not sure what to expect, but what did happen surprised me.

The giant stood behind Jones and pulled his head back sharply, so he stared at the ceiling. His eyes were wide with terror, yet the giant held him fast. One of the naked women held the ivory horn aloft, the point downwards and slowly placed it into his mouth. The horn was narrow, flaring out at the base but only to the width of three fingers. Jones's eyes widened further as she pushed the horn further and he convulsed as it passed the back of his throat. Her face was impassive as she proceeded deeper, and Jones knelt impaled like a sword swallower at a circus.

The rest of the crew of the Hyperion watched on, mostly silent but some whimpering as their fate was unfolded to them. Another woman stepped forward, holding her jug aloft and tipped the contents into the end of the horn. I assumed that the horn was hollow and that there was a hole at the other end, as there was an inordinate amount of liquid tipped in. The horn was removed, slowly as not to tear the insides of Jones.

'The drug needs to be inserted into the stomach to be at its most effective.' Kola Nor explained.

Jones screamed. The sound increased along with the pitch and he convulsed so much that I thought he would tear his arms from his body. He doubled up in pain and then threw his head back. I blinked, my eyes deceiving me or so I thought. He was changing, his hair started to thicken, and I could no longer see his scalp through it. His back seemed to lose some of its musculature. His face was altering as well, the jawline softening and also the stubble was disappearing. If I was not mistaken, it seemed as if his features were becoming more feminine.

The giant behind cut the ropes holding Jones and he slipped to the floor, curling up as if a baby in the womb. He rolled and reeled until he lay, spent and exhausted, no longer he but she. Jones rolled over, her breasts full and her hips plump. Whatever vestiges of manhood had been stripped away leaving an angel of beauty. She sobbed gently; the pain of the transformation still present.

Kola Nor nodded again, and the rest of the crew of the Hyperion were set upon, a giant behind each one and two women in front. They struggled, aware now of their punishment and that it wasn't just to be the five minutes that it took for Jones to transform. They looked anxiously to the women who carried out their tasks impassively, the same women who had held and hugged the giants brazenly. The same women who had previously knelt in their positions.

The same realisation struck me and I ran from the temple. I looked about frantically and then saw her, sitting on the bottom step of the temple. I approached and heard her sobbing. I knelt in front and held my hands out, taking hers in them. She lifted her head, her eyes meeting mine and blushed.

'You?' I felt there was no need of any further question.

She nodded and went to speak. I bade her speak not, placing my finger on her warm lips.

'No need to offer an explanation. My Clara awaits me, that I know, and I promised to stay truthful to her, and that I will. She is my soul mate and I could never deceive her. But I set out to rescue you and you have now returned the favour and for that I am eternally grateful.' She sobbed still but I could see that my words were starting to have an effect.

'What or who we were is no longer important. It is who we are now and who we will be is what we will be ultimately measured by. I was looking at a change of occupation, this wide world needs an adventurer, and this adventurer needs a partner. Will you come with me and return to Port Stuart? We can start afresh and earn fame and fortune, returning to England rich beyond belief. What say you?'

She smiled again, squeezing my fingers.

'One thing though. I cannot call you Gwa Gia. It seems unfair to remind you more of this island. And I cannot call you what you were called before.'

'What do you suggest then?' she asked. There was only one that that sprang to my mind.

'How about Boo?' I asked.

'Why Boo?' she asked.

'No reason.' I smiled.

. . .

LATER THAT DAY, we set sail in a small airship, heading away from Kola T'ui. I had found some clothes for Boo, so she didn't appear such a temptress. Kola Nor had sent us away with certain treasures. The first was a small chest of gems, which would have equated to a lifetime's wage as an airshipman in Her Britannic Majesty's Airship Corps. The second was an engine that had been fitted to the airship to replace the original small steam engine. This seemed to be of an otherworldly technology that Kola Nor explained would run without the need for stoking or shoveling fuel into it. The third treasure was the one I left with, Boo. The start of a friendship and adventures that I could have only dreamt of when I had first left Maulden.

I will write further of those adventures soon.

Yours sincerely,

Abelard Grey.

7
―――

Encounter at Port Stuart

This is the continuance of the journal of Abelard C. Grey, born and raised in the village of Maulden, Bedfordshire, in the year of our Lord 1842. This account comes from the year 1863, a year that saw the opening of the wonders of the underground. For one so used to having travelled in the clean air of the open sky, the depths of the Metropolitan Underground seem stygian in comparison, the passengers milling about like a colony of termites. Oh, to be without confines, as free as a bird. Yet, I digress. Of course, at that point, being in the Antipodes, I had no experience of such things.

Having helped rescue the beauty called Gwa Gia (and, I should note, having been rescued by the one and same wondrous creature) from her former Masters at the Isle of Kola T'ui, we fled to the relative safety of Port Stuart, a small trading town on the northern coast of Australia. Kola Nor, the giant who had carried out a dreadful punishment upon my former Captain and crew, had furnished me with three treasures, but had commanded me never to return to the Isle unbidden.

Unwilling to question my new companion upon her past life, had left the conversation terribly one-sided. I am sure that Boo, my new name for Gwa Gia - as her fiery demeanour reminded me of the stories of the Iceni queen of lore, Boudicca, had grown weary of my tiresome voice. She remained, however, in thrall at my stories and tales of my experiences. I wondered how much of the world she had seen before Kola T'ui had wrenched her masculinity and innocence from her.

Boo twirled upon the paved stones of the main street of Port Stuart. The buildings that towered above on either side amazed her innocent eyes and I thought back to the time when I first witnessed the spectacle of foreign climes. Whilst Australia was still a colony of Her Majesty's Empire, there was a great and wonderful influence from the Oriental North.

The colours of the buildings, the drapes and canopies of the small market stalls that threatened to overspill on the paved road were excitement to my own eyes, and I had seen the marvels of, say, New Orleans or Paris. Birds in ornate bamboo cages tweeted and sang, whilst monkeys on chains chattered away to passers-by. The smells of the stalls that had sold cooked food earlier in the day still lingered, brushing my nostrils and reminding me of my own hunger.

As well as the oriental influence, the impact of the Great British Empire was clear to see. Despite the oppressive humidity, gentlemen passing-by kept with the tradition of wearing hats and jackets, their fingers occasionally moving to their collars, inching their way between starched fabric and clammy skin to alleviate the discomfort. Ladies bustled along, their dresses a sea of colour amongst the dull grey and black of the men's attire.

It wasn't just the fashion that had crept to Terra Australis.

The clanks and groans made by the steam powered mechanical horses that pulled the Stephenson Cabs echoed along the street. The occasional blast of a steam whistle assaulted the ears as the cabbies blew warnings to the urchins who charged in and out, rantum scootum-like, of the crowd. I looked up, a small mail packet sailed overhead, its small engines leaving a smudge of charcoal across the canvas of the sky.

"This is astonishing, Abelard, truly wondrous," she clutched my arm and giggled, oblivious to the fact that she was acting unladylike. I should not have been surprised knowing what I did. I ventured a question, my stomach churning as I uttered the words.

"How long did you spend on Kola T'ui, Boo?" She gazed up momentarily with those large, brown eyes, catching my own staring at her. Then she tore her gaze away, her eyes closing and her head dropping.

"That is of no importance, Abelard. What was, has gone, and the only thing that matters is 'what is and will be'. You said that yourself, back on the Isle. Of my time there, and before, I do not wish to speak, that much is sure. Not until it is time." Then she was back, the chestnut eyes alight with fire and joy. "Just explain and show every new experience to me as if I was a virgin. Teach and show me the world, Abelard." She noticed my cheeks tinge at her choice of words, and she giggled again.

I became more conscious of the looks from passers-by, the sideways glances of ladies and their supposed gentlemen. The men jealous of Boo's beauty and her innocent disregard for virtue, whilst the women were disproving of such a harlot. Whilst I had found clothes for her in the ship that Kola Nor had gifted us, that by the way, we had christened *The Iceni* for obvious reasons, they were geared towards the more male form. I had hoped that they would cover her beguiling figure, however, with the addition of a corset over the basest of uniform breeches and undershirt, the enchantress had been elevated to a new circle. As I noticed the effect that Boo had on the other denizens of Port Stuart, I realised that she did too.

"Why is everyone looking at us. Am I doing something wrong?"

I was tempted to answer truthfully and chide her for her behaviour, but how was she to know better? Kola Nor had no use of a debutante who could walk demurely and converse with clergy and nobility. I took her hands and, as I stared into her eyes, for a moment, I was lost in those burnished pools.

"No, Boo. If you are being yourself, there is no need to change." I noticed she was still a little hesitant, so I carried on. "They believe you to be a little unladylike."

"Oh," she blushed slightly. "Is that bad? Can I learn to be ladylike?"

"Well, a finishing school for young ladies might help, but by all accounts, I think you would find that the most uninteresting and humdrum few years of your life."

We walked on, her small hands clutching my arm. She returned any withering glance with one of her own, the look of disdain evident from beneath the brow of the tricorn hat she wore. Her raven-black tresses flowed over her shoulders and back. Even though I should have felt comfortable, after all, my new friendship with Boo was blossoming, something was clawing at the back of my mind. It was as if something was watching us from afar, or rather, from nearby. Eyes burrowed into the back of my neck, reminding me of the feeling I often experienced from my sergeant during my training at RAC Deptford. It was clear that Boo felt it too. She shivered.

"Such an odd sensation, Abelard. I feel that someone is watching us."

"I feel it too. I find it best in these situations not to draw attention to the fact that we are aware that we may be being surveyed."

"Does it happen to you often?" she asked, clutching my arm

a little tighter. I would have been lying if I said that I wasn't exhilarated. This was my raison d'etre as our French cousins would say, my reason to be. When danger stalked me or lurked ahead in the dark, that was when I was most alive. It was my opium. I decided though, it wasn't fair to my companion to tell her this.

"It can do, but most times it is unwarranted. I put it down to a mild case of paranoia."

"But we both felt it." I was silent for a few seconds. Without making it obvious, I scanned the area ahead for any signs of danger though I was sure that it was following rather than waiting ahead. My hand patted the comforting shape of my pistol within its holster under my coat.

The benefit of hindsight is there for all but the blind to see. If I had known at that time the evil that stalked us, then would I have acted differently? I think so, but how different the outcome would have been is only for one to guess.

Leachood.

I could sense them as soon as they set foot on the dock. The dock that stood upon my land. The land that I had hunted on for centuries. Their auras glowed white hot upon the dull grey of the surroundings. Brighter than I had seen for many a year. An indication of the deeds they had accomplished already in their lives or those they will do in the future.

I breathed in, feeling their essence enter my nostrils and enticing me further. I could feel my body and soul ache to taste them. The male was younger and carried himself with an air of authority and confidence. The female was different. Her aura told me that she was older, but her appearance declared otherwise to my eyes.

I followed them as they wound their way from their airship to the Portmaster's Offices and waited. I watched from the tower of the church that stood on the dockside. A nice touch of irony that I often enjoyed. The truth of the matter was that the church, built some seventy years ago, gave the best vantage point to oversee the whole area.

I noticed the auras of others as they walked by, but they paled into insignificance before those of the couple. Eventually they left and made their way back through the throng of the market goers that attended the stalls that preyed on the visitors that arrived from all corners of their Empire. I followed at a distance; their auras easy for me to follow.

Yet there were others who had the same idea. Six men, denizens of the underworld were following the pair too. A pair kept pace with them on either side whilst the final two stalked behind. Six ugly brutes, their auras non-existent. As black as the very pits of Hell themselves. A place that I was acquainted with all too well.

"Boo, there are two men to our left. They look as undesirable as my previous crew, and they have been watching us continuously since I spotted them." I marvelled at the way that she danced around in front of me, spinning several times to end up clutching my over arm. Demurely, she looked up into my eyes and smiled.

"I see them. One with a blue shirt and a bandana, the other with white hair in a queue. Both armed with cutlasses and pistols." How she could gather that information whilst pirouetting like a ballerina astounded me. Yet she went further.

"There are two more on the opposite side, white shirts and bandoliers."

I nodded before answering.

"No doubt there will be some behind us as well. Are you armed, Boo?" I knew that she had a short rapier by her side, I was referring more to a sidearm.

"I am, though it has been some time since I fired a pistol in anger. I do have this though." She held her left arm up in front of my face to show a golden bracelet wrapped around her dainty wrist. It was a solid band of gold and from where I was standing, I couldn't see how it was fixed, as it was too tight to fit over her hand.

"Another present from Kola Nor," she explained further, but I was none the wiser.

"Hopefully, your marksmanship will come back to you. We are close to *The Iceni*, so they must make their move soon. Perhaps we should draw them out just ahead, that part of the dock is near to empty so there will be less chance of innocents being caught up in the melee."

"If that is a possibility, then maybe we should make a stand here. They might add more protection, or at the very least, a distraction?" It was the manner that she said it that shocked me. Completely impassive.

"Boo!" I exclaimed. "That is Kola Nor speaking!" She reddened, realising that she had overstepped and upset me.

"I am so sorry, Abelard. I know I have many steps still to make on this journey of rehabilitation. I will always follow your guidance." Those eyes swallowed me up again and I acquiesced, aware that I should not suppress her ideas and initiative. It was true that I had taken the role of mentor and guide, however I still saw her as an equal in our partnership. As much as I saw myself as a mentor, that equilibrium told me that Boo was my guide as well. Her advice and ideas would, I assured myself, prove invaluable in many situations.

"We both have many steps to take, so do not let it play on your mind." I smiled, hoping that I had managed to mask the worry that pounded my mind. Outnumbered thrice over, we would be lucky to survive. We carried on, approaching the quieter area of the dock ahead.

"Avast!" The cry came from behind as soon as we stepped foot on the near deserted area. Here, the dock was wooden, and the oak timbers ran straight ahead towards *The Iceni* in the distance. My heart jumped to my throat, and I swallowed it back down again and nervously took a step forward into the clearing. A shot cracked out and we both leapt forward and turned about. For a split second, the reverberation of the shot brought a deathly silence to the dock. Then panic ensued as the few bystanders there were raced for cover.

The leader of our pursuers was tall and, in a word, ugly. His nose was hooked and his grin more toothless than toothed. His greying hair, no doubt the same colour as his heart, was pulled back tightly and tied in a tail behind his head. A scar bisecting his face completed the grotesque picture. One hand held aloft a pistol that pointed to the skies, the other held a boarding axe. He called again, his voice almost as loud as the pistol shot that he had unleashed a few seconds earlier.

"Avast, I say! Hand over the woman."

His companion stepped forward into the sanctity of our clearing and pointed his sabre towards me.

"Iron Turner wants his property back," he said. Iron Turner was a sorter, one who would source anything your heart desired – and your wallet could afford. More often than not, these commodities might be intangible; the opportunities that may arise from the demise of a business rival, for example. Or the brief feeling of fulfilment after the vengeance of a wrongdoing. In the matter of Boo, it had been collateral. Or rather, she had been the collateral, being the 'map' to the Isle of Kola T'ui and the riches that it contained. Harriman and his abominable crew had paid the price, and had nearly dragged me along with them. Now, no doubt, Iron Turner wanted Boo back, to pass her on to the next unsuspecting treasure seeker, all for a handsome price.

As my hand strayed to draw my pistol, and the gargoyle that oversaw the brigands started to lower his. Before my fingers clasped around the leather grip, I was staring down the gaping muzzle of his pistol. The sands of time stood still within Chronos's hourglass.

Leachood

I saw them ahead as I alighted on the deck of the dock. In my haste, the landing was slightly heavy, and I noticed several of the inconsequential passers-by glance in my direction at the sound. Naturally, they saw nothing more than a haze where I stood, their eyes and minds a thousand or more generations behind the evolution of mine. Unaware of the presence of one so superior, they closed their minds and went on about their day.

I followed on, slipping past those who stood or walked in my way, and I approached the scene of the impending skirmish ahead. I was still some way behind them when I sensed a fracture in the time stream ahead. My consciousness stretched ahead, racing through the time streams to a moment that is yet to happen.

Two cracks rent the air one after the other. The female leaps forward and a burst of gold light splits from her wrist as she dives in front of her mate in response to the first crack that shatters the tableau below. She stands Amazonesque with her wrist held high, a golden sun radiating from it, a shield of light that blocks the path of the bullet from the leader's pistol.

The second crack sounds, so close that it appears to many as an echo of the first. The male is thrown backwards as an explosion of carmine erupts from his chest and back. He lands on his back a full two yards behind him. I watch as the female turns, her eyes widening as a scream emerges from her mouth.

I am already rewinding the time stream to my present and following the trajectory of the bullet to its origin. There, a marksman on top of the building behind me! I am there within seconds rising in front of the sailor as he peers down the sights mounted on top of his rifle's barrel. Shoving the *barrel to one side, I show my true form. His eyes widen in terror and alarm as my demonic appearance terrifies him. The shot cracks out again, this time, the bullet is propelled way wide of the mark.*

My arm stretches out towards him, and my hand enters his chest. His mouth opens to scream then freezes as I tighten my grasp around his heart. The man's eyes darken and black dust escapes from his gaping mouth which I suck in hurriedly, eager to savour the energy of his soul, no matter how dark and evil it is. The acrid taste of evil strikes my throat before I devour it, the rush of power running through my cold veins. I stare down at his dry husk as it collapses to the roof of the building, then I turn my attention to the skirmish below.

BOO LEAPT in front of me, her arm raised high. Her bracelet gleamed in the afternoon sun and expanded into Athena's Aegis, a shield of burning gold. A crack as the leader's pistol discharged its shot brought me to my senses. The shield flashed as the bullet struck it and ricocheted away into the sky. My Boo drew her rapier and parried a blow from an opponent with as much determination as her Iceni namesake.

My fingers caressed the grip of my pistol, a Lee Enfield 59 with a four-shot clip. I pulled the stubby pistol from the holster and smoothly fired a round in the direction of an attacker. I watched almost serenely as he ducked beneath a market stall and the round shattered a pot hanging from the beams of the stall. My own cutlass was still sheathed, the stump that was my left wrist (a gift from my previous captain) proven useless in battle. It was something I made a mental note to change once we had escaped from our predicament. If we should escape from our predicament, I corrected myself.

My heart raced with the exhilaration of the skirmish, and if truth be told, a little fear. Whilst I feared death, I had no illusion that the Reaper would come for me one day. And that feeling drove me on, the excitement of battle, the rolling of die (please forgive the pun) on the gamble whether I would live or die. Do not get me wrong, I am not, nor have I ever been foolhardy within combat and my only thought that day was to avoid the clutches of the Reaper, and if possible, consign my enemies to his embrace.

Of course, these wretches had made it clear that they wanted Boo, and the only reason that one could see would be to force my new companion to guide them, or others, to Kola T'ui. And both of us knew what awaited her there.

I snapped off the three rounds remaining in my Lee Enfield in quick succession and was satisfied to see an eruption of blood from one opponent as one of the rounds shattered his shoulder. I holstered my pistol, anxious not to lose her. I should take a minute here to say that a favoured pistol or sword is one to treasure, much like a lover. One becomes accustomed to the weight, balance and synergy of a weapon and the thought of having to work again to find and become used to that with a new firearm filled me with dread.

My cutlass was drawn in a split second, however, and not a moment too soon. I clashed steel against a slightly thinner blade and watched with satisfaction as I forced my attacker back. I caught a glimpse of the Iceni Queen as she danced forward, her footwork as lithe as a ballet dancer, the blade of her rapier catching the blade of another and pushing it away. Her own blade flashed again, and the man went down holding his face. Now we were outnumbered two to one. Better odds than before battle had commenced, but still outnumbered.

We backed away, closing together. Our enemies presented themselves as a wall as they advanced upon us. Boo, aware that they needed her alive, partly covered me with her golden shield. *The Iceni* was still a hundred yards to our rear, and I fancied not our chances in a straight race towards safety.

"Like we said, give us the woman and you walk away." The scar-faced brigand announced menacingly.

I had no doubt that course of action would result in my death, along with Boo becoming Gwa Gia again. I shook my head.

"Abelard," Boo whispered. "Promise me, upon your Clara's life, that you will not let them take me alive. Promise me that."

My heart leapt to my throat. How could she ask that, I asked of myself. As soon as I did, I knew the answer why. She feared a return to the Isle, more than anything else. The thought of becoming once again a concubine to the giants that ruled the island was an anathema. The prize of several brigands to swell the ranks of workers or companions to the giants would not save her from the punishment for returning.

"You have lost two in your shenanigans so far. You may overpower us, but how many of you will we take before then? Ask yourselves that and wonder if the prize outweighs your lives." I shouted back, I hoped that my voice carried no nervousness. Two of our opponents raised their pistols as if to fire and I felt Boo creep closer, the comfort of her body tight to mine as we huddled behind her shield, felt warming. I felt guilty that possibly the last thought I could have would not be of my Clara.

But my last thought was a long time away, at least, I would not make it that day. A rush of wind sounded across the dock, lifting several of the canopies of the stalls. My heart clenched, and I could feel Boo clutch me tighter, if that were humanly possible, at the sight we witnessed.

I know not where the apparition that appeared hailed from, only that Dante's Seventh Circle was a possibility, with the third Ring a distinct probability as it was, without exception, a crime against God and Nature. Its appearance was heralded by a cloud of black, inky smoke, from whence the cacodaemon finally emerged. I lowered my cutlass as the form took shape, a full ten feet high – the broadness of its shoulders seemed to engulf the wall made by our assailants. Scores of spines and horns adorned its face and upper arms, and each arm ended with a taloned claw. Smoke rose in columns from the oak timbers on which it stood, its cloven hoofs searing the wood, turning it black. The stench of sulphur assaulted out nostrils, burning deep within our throats and causing Boo to cough.

Our assailants sensed something was wrong as they noticed our reaction. The pair in the centre turned slowly to face the Hell that was behind them. And then, as if to bring further horror upon us, the demon spoke.

"I have come to feast, and you will sustain me with your essence. You have energy that I must consume and sate myself on. Believe me, it is not personal. Your auras are all that I require." The words terrified us all and Boo and I involuntarily took a step backwards. One step, but it was one step closer to our sanctuary of *The Iceni*. One of the attackers mangled a half-hearted prayer as he fell to his knees in front of the aberration.

"Yes!" The demon seemed to be in rapture. "Pray to your God. He is impotent in this matter. It will not help you, but your fear will only add taste to your aura." It stretched out a hand, and whilst I could not see as the unfortunate wretch blocked my view, I was sure that its claws penetrated the man's chest. He started to scream but the sound died to a rattle as his body shook in pain. As his lungs breathed their last breath, a cloud of black dust was expelled into the air. The dust was drawn towards the demon's mouth, and it closed its eyes as the aura was savoured.

The man withered, much like an apple left in the sun and collapsed to the ground as the demon withdrew its talons. The look of sheer terror on his parched face remains etched into my mind until this very day. I remember wondering if the dried husk would blow away in the afternoon breeze, such was the level of dehydration. The demon opened its eyes and stared straight at Boo and me.

"Leave. It is not your time today. Your auras are as yet unfilled, but I can see within the time streams that they will become purer and more complete within time. In your future, I will seek you out. Your aura will bring more nourishment in the future than at this point in the streams. It will be much more satisfying."

My heart hammered away, a fast and furious tattoo. Our eyes met across the short distance, and I was even more glad of that extra step we had taken. I felt my skin crawl within the presence of the foul beast. I could tell that Boo felt the same. We watched, mesmerised, as the demon despatched another of our attackers. The leader of the gang now stood and emptied the magazine of his pistol at the beast. The rounds sank into the flesh with a hiss. Tendrils of smoke rose into the sky from the open wounds that shrank and disappeared as they healed over.

"Go!" The demon demanded. "I may not be able to control my urges - and I do hate when that spoils my nourishment."

Boo tore herself away from my grasp and pulled at my arm.

"Come, Abelard. You heard its warning!"

I turned and ran with Boo. We made it to *The Iceni* in a matter of seconds and as we stood at the top of the gangplank to the airship gifted from Kola Nor, we saw the beast despatch the last assailant in the same manner as the others. The beast rose over the dock and turned its head towards us.

"Boo! Start the engines."

"With pleasure, Captain!"

I decided to make no remark to Boo over her impertinence - we had long decided that there was no need for ranks between us. Equals, one and all. As she bolted below deck to get *The Iceni* moving, I stared at the abomination as it moved slowly towards us. I could see the anguish on its face as it fought its own demonic desire and need to feed with that of its honour in keeping its word in allowing us to escape. Escape, if only to nurture and grow our auras with heroic deeds until such a time that it could find us again. I raised a hand in salute to the demon, who had after all, saved us. It could have easily taken us there and then, reducing us to a dry husk and leaving us to disintegrate in the wind at Port Stuart.

I was not shocked to see the demon stop and raise a taloned claw in mimicry of my own salute. My body reeled in nauseousness as I realised that at some point in our future, Boo and I would encounter the abomination again. I would be a liar if I said that thought caused me no trepidation or fear.

I could feel the rumble of the powerful, other-worldly engines as they fired up and I turned upon my heel and stalked away to the 'quarterdeck', which is to say, the cabin from which we commanded and steered *The Iceni*. Boo was already lifting *The Iceni* from its mooring and steering us away from Port Stuart.

Neither of us could find the words to describe what had happened, nor did we feel the need to. Our collective thought was only to leave and never return. Our destination was unknown at present, and the possibilities were endless with the technology on *The Iceni*. I strode to the captain's table and withdrew a bottle of ruby port from the pedestal cupboard along with two crystal glasses. The thick, red liquid did little to deaden the emotional anguish that we had endured with our brush with the Reaper.

With quickening speed, we headed away from the setting sun and to the safety of the open skies and ocean to the East, leaving Port Stuart and its dock of demons and dried husks behind.

8

The Ziggurat of Sunat Tow.

I write this account of the strange and sometimes terrible happenings at the Ziggurat of Sunat Tow, a ruin of some antiquity upon a long-forgotten isle in the seas around Timor. It was in the latter part of the year of our Lord 1863. Once again, I can only give assurances as to the premise of each conversation rather than the exact words uttered at the time. I have never been one for the memory of dialogue, especially after so many years – but my retentiveness of occurrences – perhaps helped by the dramatic and fantastic nature of the same – is *nulli secundus*, or second to none.

Part, the First.
In which an island is approached, a hostility sours the air and a marriage, or opposition to one, and various letters are discussed.

"Land ahoy!" I called and rang the ship's bell that hung on the main deck. From where I stood under the gasbag of *The Iceni*, shielded from the merciless beating of the tropical sun, I could see las Isla de los Muertos, the so-called Island of the Dead break the horizon. The shadow cast by the gasbag, though, gave no respite from the humidity that threatened to drown me. My erstwhile companion, Boo, rose from where she had sat and leapt nimbly onto the gunwale of *The Iceni*, holding on to one of the ropes that held the gasbag to the airship.

"It looks much like any other coast, for one with such a dread name."

I thought back to the Isle of Kola T'ui, and the day that we had rescued each other. For reasons that have already been accounted for in earlier pages of this journal, I had been in no fit state to look at the Isle as we approached, but neither had I wanted to look back as we left in *The Iceni*. Therefore, I was not able to make a comparison between the two, yet I knew what she had meant.

"It may look like any other coast but this one's name is apt. I doubt that there is another in the world with a more well-deserved name." The voice cut in from behind us both. The first of a trio of guests had appeared, summoned by the clamour of the ship's bell. This was the Right Reverend Rutherford-Jones, a member of the clergy who did little to entice any wayward lambs back into the fold. He was a bigot and a drunkard, and was the master proponent of that wonderful maxim; 'I like what I say and I'll say what I like.'

"Yet, we still go there." Boo was cutting in her retort. The pair had not seen eye to eye since the day our journey started.

"Yes, we do. Isla de los Muertos." Rutherford-Jones stared ahead; his eyes fixed upon the smudge of greenery upon the horizon. "Your task is nearly completed, Mr Grey."

Whilst I contemplated the Reverend's words, I held my hand out to Boo, who graciously took it and alighted from the side of the ship. She made little sound as her bare feet landed upon the deck. The young woman had had several names; Gwa Gia had been her name on Kola T'ui, and I had christened her Boudicca, or Boo for short. The name, though, that she had been born with was not known to me. Her raven black tresses were tied back into a low ponytail that hung halfway down her back. A white silk shirt billowed out like a sail in full wind over her midshipman style breeches. The mass of black and coloured tattoos that covered her back, shoulders and torso were visible through the thin material.

"Don't worry, Mr Grey. I am a man of my word. Your payment is safe right here." He patted the breast pocket of his jacket. The price he was willing to pay for our assistance was high, not in gold or money, but in testimonials and letters of commendation. These I would need to absolve me of complicity in my previous Captain's crimes. Despite a letter of marque and a commission to act as a privateer for Her Britannic Majesty's Airship corps, Captain Harriman, had overstepped the line on several occasions, infringing upon the neutrality of several countries and causing Her Majesty quite some embarrassment. I could not, and would not, set foot upon England's green and pleasant land whilst under such a mark. I could not let my beloved Clara, my betrothed and one so innocent beyond compare, see me arrested and chained and brought before a court martial. The likelihood of which would see me end up dancing a jig from a yardarm at dawn. It was imperative that I clear my name, hence I found myself enduring the company and occasional diatribe from God's Little Napoleon.

"Of that, I have no doubt, Reverend." I turned to face the older man. Shorter than even Boo, with a face so marked by the redness of rosacea, that it was as if the character of the

Summoner had been lifted from the pages of The Canterbury Tales, and now stood before me. Uncomfortable and at unease in this climate, he gave an air of aloofness. Indeed, he had kept himself separate from us all where he could, even dining apart for most of the journey. About his neck was the badge of his office, the clerical collar - or dog collar as it is now more commonly known.

"And your daughter?" I enquired. "This is where she is? Of that, are you sure?"

"Of course. Sophia had written several times of her intent to investigate the ruins of the Temple of Sonat Tow on the island. She studied archaeology under Professor Carlleyle and was well versed on the subject."

"And as her father, you had no issue with her choice of profession. I mean to say, the world is not a safe place, especially the less civilised areas where such antiquities and sites are to be found."

"Even a fool who keeps silent is considered wise. You will do well to hold your tongue, Mr Grey. I do not need a lecture from you or anyone on what sort of a parent I have been. Sophia is her own woman." I expected him to see him froth at the mouth. "I will return to my cabin for the time being. Please send word when we break the coast." With that he turned and withdrew from the deck.

"Hopefully, this is the beginning of the end for this awkward journey." Boo spoke softly beside me. Before I could answer, there was a cough from behind us.

We both turned to find the quiet and unassuming figure of Darrowby, manservant to the Reverend, and the second of our three passengers. He stood, ramrod straight, dressed impeccably in a waistcoat and tails. How the Dickens the swell didn't just melt in this sun I do not know. We stared at him, aware that we were both blushing at Boo's awkward choice of words.

"Do not judge the man too harshly, Miss Boo. Sophia is his

pride and joy, second only to his church that is. He raised her to be independent and strong-willed, and that is certainly what the young lady is." Darrowby's slight London accent came through when he spoke. His tone was more matter of fact than apologetic for his employer. He continued. "Reverend Rutherford-Jones has always been one to be in the limelight, and his reputation is extremely important to him. Hence this rush to collect her in time for her wedding. It would be best to duck when she is finally safe on board. Sophia will not take kindly to having her studies pulled from underneath her, and the Reverend was extremely irritated by her lack of respect for her duty and to her future husband."

"If she is as strong-willed and independent as you say, why would her father take exception to her wanting to exercise that independence?" Boo asked.

"There are two reasons for that. Firstly, because of who her fiancé, Mr Norton is, or rather, who Mr Norton's father is. There is an element of pressure from his family. Secondly, do you remember when I mentioned the Reverend is one to be in the limelight? By having his Sophia wed Norton, his standing in the city will be sky-high. So, this is all about gaining face."

"Norton's father is…?" For a few seconds I couldn't place the name. Then, with a groan, I realised who our third passenger was.

"Field Marshall Sir John Norton, 5th Earl of Newton Moreton." We both said together. Field Marshall Norton, Commander of Her Britannic Majesty's Armies, one of the most powerful men in the Empire. And I had unknowingly allowed his son on board *The Iceni*. My heart twisted as if Field Marshall Norton had gripped it in his clawlike grasp.

Darrowby nodded. He fidgeted slightly, raising a hand to stroke his cheekbone under his right eye with the pad of his forefinger. I had only known him for the duration of the journey so far, yet it seemed a very uncharacteristic movement from the valet. It may have been that *The Iceni* was nearing her destination, with Rutherford-Jones and his party moving towards uncertainty and possible danger. Or, more than likely, he was hiding something. I made a mental note to ensure I spread the flats with him if the opportunity arose. If that was his 'tell', then Darrowby and his money could well be parted in a game of cards.

"What is it, Darrowby? If there is something else, you must tell me. If we are heading towards danger, then I must know more, for all of our sakes." I half turned and jabbed a finger towards Isla de los Muertos. My new left hand shone as the sun caught it, a wonderful piece of engineering courtesy of an old friend. It was constructed of brass, steel and gold and was fitted closely over the stump of my left hand, cruelly blown to smithereens by my old crewmates. With a little practise I was now able to grip and clench tools and weapons with almost the same dexterity as the hand I had been born with.

"I cannot say, Mr Grey. It is privileged information."

"You must, man!"

I could see the conflict on the valet's face. He didn't want to betray the trust of his employer yet there was something else. Something deep.

"It is not something I normally do; indeed, I have never looked at a master's correspondence before. A month ago, the Reverend received a letter that drove him temporarily deranged, to the point that I feared for his safety." Darrowby rubbed his cheek again. Something still wasn't right. I felt Boo's hand rest on my forearm.

"He bade me wave down a cab, and whilst he normally distrusts new-fangled automation, preferring traditional horse and cab, he stressed urgency, even if it was one of Stephenson's horseless carriages. He went straight to Norton's house in Belgravia and didn't return until late in the evening." I implored him silently to continue, fearing that we might break the coast before he finished his anecdote.

"It is regret that I now admit to breaking his trust. He was in such distress that I wondered what had caused it. In his haste, he had left the letter upon his desk and, curiosity getting the better of me, I read it.

"It was from Sophia. In it, she expressed her desire to carry on her work at the Temple of Sonat Tow. She also stated that she had no wish to proceed with her marriage to Mr Norton, and that she had no intention of returning. It was very simply put. No ambiguity, no acknowledgement of his time as her father and absolutely no apology." Boo pressed my forearm lightly as he spoke, telling me that she had noticed something from the conversation, though at the time I had no inkling what she had seen.

"So, this is not a mission of rescue and repatriation but one of abduction?" I asked.

"That I do not know, I think maybe, that between them, they mean to convince her to return to England."

"Is that what you hope, Darrowby?" Boo questioned. I looked at her, as there was something unsaid in her words.

"I think that is what they mean to do, Miss Boo. Though I do not know. Now I must return below decks to attend to the Reverend." He bowed his head slightly then retired.

I looked at Boo, gazing into those dark brown eyes. What had they seen? What subtle clues had Darrowby given away?

"He is not telling us the whole truth, Abelard."

"How so?"

"The way he spoke when he disclosed the details of the letter. It was not just sadness, there was something else. I noticed an emotion I wasn't expecting, one of pride or even success." She hesitated before adding, "or was it hope?"

That look had eluded me, I know, but I had seen similar on Boo. A look of pure emotion in direct juxtaposition to the situation to hand. Tasked by her master, the giant Kola Nor, to travel the world and find undesirables who would sell their own grandmother to have a chance at gaining the elusive treasure of Zheng Jing, hidden for centuries on the Isle of Kola T'ui, my previous Captain, the black-hearted blaggard Harriman had come to hold her captive. She had been instructed to withhold the location of the island from the likes of Harriman for as long as possible, in order to make the information appear genuine, and also to find out exactly what levels of depravity these 'treasure-seekers' would sink to.

And those horrors I did indeed bear witness to. Agamemnon's crimes against the trojan princess Cassandra, or the depravity committed by the Roman procurator of Britain against Boudicca and her daughters were comparable to those committed by Harriman and his crew. Yet, when Boo finally marked the Isle of Kola T'ui on the map, I didn't see anger, horror or shock on her face. I saw victory. Victory because her master's plan had been achieved despite her torture, and a fresh cadre of ne'er-do-wells was on the way to swell the ranks of slaves on the island..

"What is going on here, Boo?" I asked

My companion shook her head and turned her head to once again look upon the approaching land.

"I am not sure, Abelard. But with the current speed and weather conditions, we will know more in two hours."

Although we were not to accompany the others to the temple, we attired and equipped ourselves as if we were. Boo favoured her breeches, but preferred to wear them with heavy riding boots, despite the climate. A dark blue double-breasted frock-coat completed her attire, worn over a silk shirt and leather corset ensemble. A short rapier fastened in a sheath at her waist accompanied the two Webley & Scott pistols that sat holstered upon her extremely feminine hips.

In comparison, I wore the faded, waxed gentleman's overcoat that had seen me through many an adventure, over a waistcoat that held extra clips for my Lee Enfield pistol. The balance of my attire was that of the true colonial soldier, the drab, and cheerless khaki drill. It was not of love of the colour or hue, or some nostalgia for the time in which I had taken the Queen's Shilling – that being only a few years past. It was for the comfort that the fabric leant in the sweltering heat.

We waited on deck as *The Iceni* broke the coastline and headed for the Temple of Sunat Tow. Our guests came on deck, first Darrowby and the Reverend, then our third guest, James Norton.

I regarded him as he strode across to his father-in-law to be. He was tall, taller than me by a head, and his golden hair was extremely well groomed, as was the moustache so favoured by officers of Her Majesty's Army. He held himself as someone who had led others into the jaws of Hell and back again - and there was an air about him that showed he would do it again if needed.

He may well have been born from the imagination and talent of a master such as Michaelangelo or Titian, or when the light fell correctly, born from the loins of Zeus and Hera themselves. Apollo personified, he had to stoop when he carried himself twixt the threshold and the head jamb of the cabin doors. He had embarked carrying a soldier's duffel bag on one shoulder, the drab khaki crammed to bursting point. Gripped in his other hand had been a large bore hunting rifle. A long telescopic sight the length of my forearm sat on top of the rifle.

He was, as I was, now all attired in khaki; trousers held up by white braces, gaiters and loose shirt, with a set of blancoed webbing crossing his back. The same rifle was slung over his shoulder, its weight and size a mere inconvenience to the hero. Other small arms, including a burnished machete, were attached to his belt. He turned and looked at me, nodding to indicate something behind me.

"By all accounts, if the missives from Sophia are correct, then the temple should be on the reverse slope of that mountain. If you would be so kind to drop us right on top, Mr Grey."

I nodded and looked at Boo, who started to retire to the wheelhouse to make amendments to the course. It seemed as she was desperate to remove herself from the deck and the discerning look of Rutherford Jones. Alas, she did not make it in time.

"And on dead men ye shall not cut your flesh, neither ye shall make to you any figures, *either marks in your flesh*; I am the Lord," the hoary voice of the Reverend broke the silence. "Leviticus 19:28." he went on to explain. If the Right Reverend had stilled his tongue for a few seconds more, allowing Boo to gain the sanctity of the wheelhouse, then all may have been well. But Boo heard, though Rutherford-Jones had not endeavoured to speak sotto voce. Indeed, there were natives on neighbouring islands who may have heard the bigoted rumblings from the old man. Boo had stood tall, placing her hands upon her hips and thrusting her chest out.

"If your right eye offends thee, pluck it out and cast it aside!" She had stared straight at the Reverend, standing her ground. Boudicca incarnate, her figure the perfect channel for the fury of the centuries dead Iceni warrior queen. Rutherford-Jones had stammered and spluttered, unused to be defied and confronted. His hands shook as he brought himself under control, then he blustered.

"Jezebel! You are nothing but the Mother of Harlots! The Mystery of Babylon, a plague upon you for your fornications and you, . . . "he turned to address me but couldn't find an insult such was the shock. "You should know better, Mr Grey! You should know better."

And in truth, I did know better. I knew that I should not have placed my future is the hands of one such as the Reverend at the expense of my companionship with Boo. Of my time taking the Queen's Shilling, along with my life as a free soaring adventurer, I should have known that there is always another way. That is the way that I should have sought, rather than be blinkered like a racehorse by the prospect of an easy return to the motherland and into the arms of my beloved, Clara. But for now, I bit my tongue.

"In less than sixty heartbeats, you will be off *The Iceni,* and I will be overjoyed" continued the fiery Boo, unwilling to backdown.

"Yourself and me both, young lady! Although, you may have forgotten that there is a return journey to be made," he patted his breast pocket, "that is, if your captain wants his pass back to England."

"If it was my decision, then our journey would end when you disembark. You would be better suited here in the jungle with snakes and other crawlies to be your companions." She spat on the deck between them and stared defiantly, hands thrust upon hips like a diminutive imitation of the Colossus of Rhodes. Rutherford-Jones snapped, raising his hand as if to deliver a slap. It was left to myself and Norton to disarm the situation.

"Reverend, we must remember Sophia. Your daughter is who we should consider, and we are that close to reaching her." He motioned with his thumb and forefinger. His father-in-law-to-be seethed but slowly calmed and lowered his hand.

"Boo, please attend to the wheel." She stared at me, her eyes burning into mine; twin misericords twisting into me. I felt the unspoken question that her glare posed - this Clara, was this beauty worth this pain? She spun on her heels and left the deck. Within seconds, we felt *The Iceni* respond to her commands, as she first banked, then started to sink towards the jungle canopy below.

The canopy broke to reveal a giant ziggurat, the stones of which were covered in moss, lichens and vines, so much so, that the temple was barely discernible as such. Four giant towers rose from each corner, pointing to the heavens in an offensive affront to Rutherford-Jones's God. On the higher most level could be seen the canvas tents of Sophia's excavation team.

Expertly, Boo lowered the vessel until the hull was nigh six feet above the top of the ziggurat. Norton looked overboard, then nodded in appreciation at the dextrous skill of my pilot. Grabbing the disembarking ladder, he threw the end of the thick rope ladder over the side. Then the unthinkable happened. It was truly a majestic sight, looking back in hindsight, but at that time, shocking and horrifying indeed.

Four beams of incandescent blue light shot from each tower, meeting at a point high above *The Iceni*'s gasbag. A sharp crack split the silence, sending swarms of birds to the air from the canopy, and causing all four of us to momentarily duck. I was reminded of the Aurora Australis as the light cascaded down to form a screen around *The Iceni*, trapping the airship within its confines.

"What in the blazes! Wait here!" I called out and ran to the wheel house.

"What is that?" Boo had instinctively slammed the alien engines into hold and was peering anxiously from the windows of the wheel house, trying to gauge where the light screen was. I didn't have to tell her to keep the airship from making contact with the shimmering blue folds of light.

"Boo! You stay with the ship and maintain a safe distance from those lights. I fear that I am going to have to accompany Norton. Whilst they are convincing Sophia and her team to return, I shall endeavour to find whatever demonic conjurations have trapped us here. Hopefully I can find a way to deactivate this screen, and to free *The Iceni*."

She looked worried, afraid for the safety of both of us.

"Be careful, Abelard. There is something that the three of

them aren't telling. Do not trust them!" I could only nod, then returned to the others. Norton was ready to descend the rope ladder, a pistol in hand. Not a small stubby pistol either, but a handgun that looked like it could take down a charging bull with ease. A clip of six shots sprouted from underneath the barrel. With a cheery wave, he slipped over the side from view. I bent over the side, to see him alight at the foot of the rope ladder, the pistol in one hand and his vicious looking machete in the other. He circled warily, checking each direction for threat.

Darrowby had already made for the ladder and was clambering down. He had a short-barrelled shotgun strapped to his back. Rutherford-Jones stood at the side. looking at the ladder with apprehension. His hands clung to the small satchel that was slung over one shoulder. I could only guess what was going through his mind as he eyed the ladder. He jumped as I took hold of his shoulder.

"A word of warning, Reverend. One more comment like the one you uttered earlier about my friend and comrade, and I ensure that you'll never set foot upon *The Iceni* again. I care not for the letters inside your jacket, if in the action of gaining them my friendship with Boo suffers. Now! Over the side with you - and I will see you at the bottom."

It snapped him from his reverie and quite sprightly for such an old fellow, he swung his legs over the gunwale. Wisely, he kept quiet and began his descent. I followed, checking my weapons, before grabbing the rope with my metal hand. I alighted gently at the end, and the four of us stood upon the top of the ziggurat. The stone upon which we stood, despite the centuries of disuse and encroachment by the surrounding jungle showed signs of master craftsmen. Each flagstone or block sat perfectly adjoined to its neighbour. It seemed that pushing a knife blade between them would prove to be an impossible task., yet Sophia's team had done so, managing to bivouac tents upon the top. A stone building was sited at one end of the terrace, its door leading to darkness. I shivered. For lifetimes past, how many priests had stood here and addressed kings and commoners alike? What other odious rituals had taken place on this very spot in honour of this Sunat Tow.

For all the Reverend's swagger on going overboard, he was now panting hard. I waved upwards at Boo, and she pulled the ladder up. I felt Darrowby's eyes burrow into me as he lit an oil-soaked brand with a lighter, and I knew what he was going to ask, so I answered before he had chance to speak.

"I am going to accompany you, to make sure whatever damned contraption is keeping us captive is removed so that *The Iceni* can carry us out of here. And, as for the ladder, no point in having anyone board the ship and take it whilst we are all down below. I know Boo can fight like a harridan possessed, yet she could easily be outnumbered."

Norton nodded once more, proving himself to be a man of very few words. Maybe that was why Sophia had decided to call the engagement off, realising that these dusty temples spoke more than her betrothed, just in different ways. That thought caused me to remember Boo's query above, so I felt it was now time to make an interjection.

"One moment, gentlemen." I called, tapping the side of my boot with the cutlass blade.

"What is it, Grey? Can't you see that we should be moving off?" Norton pointed his machete at the dark doorway that led down into the Stygian depths below.

"This cannot wait, Mr Norton." I, for one, had not forgotten my manners and addressed him as a gentleman ought to be addressed, whether or not I thought he was one. "My companion, Boo, has instructions to make her escape in *The Iceni* should I not return. That much should be evident. She would be unwilling to stay and save you, Reverend, if I am lost, as you both rub each other up the wrong way, so to speak. So, it would in your best interests to keep me alive and with you whilst we regain Sophia and bring that screen down."

"It seems as if you do not trust us, Grey. Why is that?" enquired Norton.

"Because it is evident that you do not trust me. There is something that you are not telling about this mission. As I am now stuck with you, and our lives and fates are intertwined, I believe that I have a right to know, and that you should have the decency to say what is what."

Norton looked across at the Reverend, whose eyes flitted from me to his son-in-law-to-be. Finally, the blond soldier sighed and sheathed the machete that he had been holding.

"You are right, Grey. We should be working together, with nothing between us. There is something that you haven't been told, and the only reason why you have been kept in the dark is, well - quite frankly, we thought you wouldn't take our commission, even with the prize at stake."

"The Reverend received a letter, from Sophia." He continued and I mentally waved him on, all too aware.

"No, not the one that Darrowby told you about. A later one, that was addressed to the Reverend and delivered to my address." He turned, half apologetically to the butler.

"You are quite loud, Darrowby. I overheard you telling Grey about the letter from my cabin."

"Reading a gentleman's correspondence, eh, Darrowby. That will be the end of your employ when we return to England." snorted Rutherford-Jones. "In the first letter, Sophia broke off our engagement. In the second, she explained why. During the excavation, she had met someone and was now betrothed to him. From her words, it is a local man," the Reverend carried on.

"Local man, be damned!" exclaimed Norton. "She thinks she is engaged to a deity, one of the pagan gods this temple was dedicated to. The girl has gone completely mad!"

"Be quiet, James! This individual clearly has some control over my daughter, and has twisted her mind for whatever iniquitous reason. I suggest we move on." With that, Rutherford-Jones made for the entrance, taking a burning brand from Darrowby, before being swallowed up by the maw. Norton glared at me, then stormed off, pushing past the butler.

"Time to get our hands dirty, Mr Darrowby. Are you ready?" I pulled my Lee Enfield Double Nine from its holster and checked the clip. Thrusting it back into the leather, I marvelled at the security I felt of its weight upon my hip. Darrowby did likewise, breaking open his shotgun, as if to reassure himself that the brass bottomed shells were still there. With a click, he closed the breach and nodded.

"Like one o'clock, Mr Grey."

I could tell he was scared. His eyes betrayed him, a nervous tic, but to his credit he didn't falter. I wondered if he had seen action at some point in the past, had he taken the Queen's Shilling? Preparing to follow his old master into the depths of a catacomb on the other side of the earth, may not have been foremost in his thoughts when he entered Rutherford-Jones's employ. Yet, he was coping admirably.

Part, the Second.
Beneath the ziggurat, in darkness and horror, where mysteries and religions long dead are discovered.

THE DARKNESS SWALLOWED us up like it had the others, and we started our journey to the lower levels of the Temple of Sunat Tow. Having spent my career on the open air and sea, I was not surprised when I felt unease in the dark confines of the passageway, despite the flickering of the torches. With the benefit of hindsight, (I am sure that foresight would make a much more beneficial skill!) it was not the claustrophobic environment that perturbed me, but the impending doom that we walked unknowingly towards.

We walked in silence, following the steps that wound downwards. The only sound was the slow drip, drip, drip of water from the ceiling. The stone of the steps were worn in places, innumerable drops of moisture over countless centuries wearing the hard granite away.

Norton stopped, waving Darrowby on to accompany the Reverend. As I drew level, he grabbed my arm. I felt the tightness of his grip through the overcoat.

"Be careful! You should ask what he carries in that infernal satchel!" He hissed in my ear. Before I could query his statement, a call from the others roused us. The urgency in the voices echoed from the stone of the stairway. We scurried down, the handle of my cutlass finding its way into the grip of my metallic claw. Though the cold metal of that 'hand' was unfeeling, I was buoyed and reassured by the feel of the pistol in my other hand.

We found ourselves entering a long chamber. Rutherford-Jones and Darrowby were a little ahead of us, towards the centre of the room. Countless drills and skirmish experience had instilled a sense of automata in myself and Norton, but the shock of what we faced, and what had caused the others to cry out, nearly led to a stumble.

Dark figures, wrapped in the torn, dusty linen of grave shrouds ambled towards us, arms held out, reaching out as if to accuse us of trespass against their broken rest. Parched skin showed where the linen was torn. Any thought that these were men who breathed was laid to rest by the foremost figure whose coverings had fallen from its face, revealing its lower mandible hanging from one side of its face. The dark pits that had once been home to eyes, seemed to bore deep into me.

A cannon let loose next to me and it took me a second to realise that it was only Norton's handgun. My head pounded as the echo of the shot reverberated about the crypt. The enclosed chamber only increased the volume. The wight was hit in the chest by Norton's projectile, the upper half of the its body was obliterated in a cloud of dust.

The remaining four were sent back to their eternal rest just as quickly. Darrowby's shotgun flashed, the strong smell of cordite rising to our nostrils from the flames of its discharge. Once more, Norton's pistol roared, with results unsurprisingly similar to before. I sidestepped the one that lurched towards me, my blade of the cutlass bearing down upon the outstretched arms. The heavy steel swept through both forearms with ease. I was somewhat relieved to see the hands fall to the floor and remain still. The beast however, howled. Its screeching voice tore into our souls until I silenced it, my metal fist driven straight into its maw.

Darrowby shivered as if something had crept over his grave. An unfortunate choice of words considering our position. His voice shook as he asked the question that we were all wanting to ask.

"What the Dickens were they?" I was surprised how he was holding up. He stared, his eyes fixed upon the far wall, as if he didn't care to see the devilish beings again. I looked at the two that Darrowby had shot; the shotgun shells had caught them low, shredding their legs. They made pitiful attempts to crawl towards us, their fingers flaking as they endeavoured to gain purchase upon the stone floor. Rattling noises interspersed with mews and shrieks emanated from their parched throats, as if they were cursing us. Norton stepped forward, casually crushing their outstretched hands to dust under his boots. Then he raised his revolver, gripping it by the long barrel, and struck one on the head. It ceased moving immediately, and the other raised its head towards

Norton and the pistol. Though it looked upon him with empty sockets, I thought I witnessed a change in its countenance as if it knew its impending second death. I sensed a feeling of relaxation and relief as it paused in its attempts to move and fell silent. Seconds later, it had been returned to dust.

Rutherford-Jones sank to his knees and gave an anguished cry. A cry of a man facing his maker for judgement. His body racked with sobs, great sobs that threatened to break his body. Disgusted, Norton snarled, brandishing his fist towards his father-in-law-to-be. "It's time you told him, Rutherford! It's time you levelled with us all and explain the real reason we are in this mess! We'll start with that satchel!"

Rutherford-Jones shrank like a naughty schoolboy under the gaze of a ferocious battle-axe of a governess. His hands gripped the leather pack, trying to push it behind him, trying to follow the old mantra; out of sight, out of mind. I decided to add my voice to Norton's, wanting to place my trust in that of a fellow warrior rather than in a man of the cloth. I pulled my own pistol from its holster and pointed the barrel towards the reverend.

"We can look now and discuss the same with you, or we can look for ourselves, reverend. Hand it over." Rutherford-Jones closed his eyes. He sighed and held out the satchel.

"Take it, Darrowby." Norton ordered, and the butler stepped forward, almost apologetically to take the bag from his master. Finally, the reverend spoke.

"Be careful with that. You don't understand what we are dealing with here."

"Well, enlighten us, Father-in-Law."

Darrowby looked first at Norton, then at me, his eyes pleading for some direction. I nodded and he slung his shotgun over his shoulder and unbuckled the straps on the leather bag.

"Forgive me Father, for I have sinned." Rutherford-Jones

spoke softly as Darrowby delved into the satchel. He withdrew his hand sharply, exclaiming loudly.

"Hallo! What the Dickens?" He blew on his fingers.

"What is the matter, Darrowby?"

"Nothing, sir. Something in here is hot!" He turned the satchel upside and shook it. Something metallic clattered to the stone, sparkling in the light from the burning brands. Our eyes were drawn towards it as moths to a lamp at night. An ornate band of gold, perhaps the width of my finger. The light of the flames flickered in numerous rubies set into the yellow metal. One piece of the band flared out to a rhombus shape, upon which was set more rubies in the form of a blood-red, crooked cross. Norton drew his machete and deftly picked the band up with the blade.

"Well, well, well. That's a fine bit of tomfoolery, if ever I saw it." Norton whistled.

"It's a coronet, or something similar. Indian from the look of that cross." I answered, spellbound at the sparkle of the sanguine gems.

"And in the End of Days, Upon the Eve of the Return of the Dark Ones, the dead will rise from their graves and sepulchres and will drag the living down to darkness. Their energy and essence will feed the Dark Ones, and the Demon Lord D'hmet will rejoice in his freedom and return." We all turned to face Rutherford-Jones, his voice stilted as if it was ready to fail. He was looking wide-eyed at the piece of jewellery dangling from Norton's machete.

"For the sake of me, I can't seem to recollect that verse from Sunday School, Reverend." I spoke softly but my words carried in the deathly silence. They jolted him from his reverie and he turned to face us, his hands wringing feverishly. Beads of perspiration sought their way down his red flushed face.

"That's because you won't find it in the Bible, Grey. Eh, Father-in-Law?" Norton reached out tentatively with his finger to touch the gold band. He withdrew it as quickly as Darrowby had.

"I said that you will not understand what you are into, you fools! Give me that back!" Rutherford-Jones scrabbled about on the flagstones, desperately reaching out for the circlet, which Norton swung tantalisingly out of reach of the old man.

"What is it, Reverend? I think we are due an explanation," I said. It was not a coincidence that I still had my revolver in my hand. I flicked open the clip to count the cartridges left, then snapped it back shut. The click echoed in the room; the sound amplified by the ancient stone. Rutherford-Jones looked nervously at the gun, then at Darrowby and Norton.

"Some half a dozen years ago, due to my high standing in the Church, I was asked to categorise some old manuscripts at the British Museum. Manuscripts of a dark nature, written down by Portuguese monks before the Raj became British. They told of ancient treasures that were devilish and pagan in nature. That circlet is one such treasure. Yes, Grey, your supposition of it being Indian is correct. The Circlet of Mahakali, the goddess of Time and Death, consort of Bhairava."

"Does your superior know of your dabbling in such blasphemous dealings?" Norton laughed. Rutherford-Jones stared back at his future son-in-law.

"When the Dark Ones return, the Almighty will stand against them. I have faith that He will be strong enough to banish them once again."

"But of course, it would help if all your eggs weren't in one basket." I added, reading between the lines.

"Balderdash, Grey!" Norton stamped his feet. "All this talk of gods and Dark Ones is enough to make a stuffed bird laugh. Preposterous!"

I looked at the old man, thoroughly humiliated on his knees, but the look in his eyes for that circlet was want, as if it was the very representation of why we had come to this god-forsaken place. Norton was no use in this argument, he himself was humiliated and embarrassed at having been deserted by his betrothed. I wondered, briefly, how I would be affected if I heard the same news from Clara. And, just as briefly, my thoughts faltered upon Boo, valiantly holding *The Iceni* in place, a matter of so many fathoms above.

"What is it, Reverend? What does this circlet do and why do you crave it so much." I held my hand up to silence Norton before he could speak. "Hush, man, let him answer."

"Mahakali is the goddess of Time and Death, you see it, don't you, Grey? She is going to marry him, become his bride. For that to happen, she has to become like him! She has to become like this Sunat Tow." His face flushed even redder, like the face of a wet lush in a gutter. Frenziedly, he grabbed my arm, his fingers pressing deep into my skin. Eyes burning deep, he shook as he spoke. "He will take her life and she will be as dead as he is!"

"No!" A stifled cry came not from Norton, but from Darrowby. Why, hallo, I thought. Boo was right, Darrowby had more to tell. My eyes flitted to Norton, who stood dispassionate and silent.

"What does this do? What is its purpose." I pointed to the ruby encrusted circlet.

"The crooked cross, or sauwastika to call it by its rightful name, is a holy symbol." Rutherford-Jones answered. "Imbued with the power of Mahakali, it can alter both Time and Death. I hope that we are in time, but if we are too late, then I hope that an older religion will bring her back to me. And in doing so, if it condemns my soul to Hell, I hope that the Almighty takes pity upon me."

"You disgust me almost as much as your trollop of a daughter does." Norton spat, throwing the circlet to the ground. It rolled across the stone towards Darrowby. The impeccably dressed man bent down and flicked it into the satchel.

"We need to leave, Grey! This instant. We need to return to Darwin and pick up a company of Grenadiers, then return here and raze this abomination to the ground."

"An interesting thought, Norton. But you are forgetting *The Iceni* is held captive up above. It will be a long walk back to the coast from here, and an even longer swim from there. And..." I paused, fixing the stronger, larger man in my gaze. "We did come here for Sophia, and that's that."

"I care not for her now, Grey. Not after this."

"But you are still an officer in Her Majesty's Army, Norton. An officer who swore an oath to Queen Vic to protect and serve, and to further the machinations of the Empire beyond its borders. Us three merry men, the Butler, the Reverend, and the Privateer are going onward. Feel free to accompany us, but be aware that I will make it known upon our return whether we had the assistance of the Army."

I turned back to Rutherford-Jones and hauled him to his feet.

"Give him the satchel, Darrowby." The butler held out the leather, anxious to be rid of the burning gold circlet.

"That was well said, Mr Grey. Thank you for your words."

"Thank me properly when we are home and dry, Darrowby. Now, one more thing." I leant in and whispered sotto voce, "How long? How long has Sophia been your infatuation? I take it the young lady knows nothing of your interest in her?" I swear he turned redder than a beetroot, his secret unleashed and a secret no more.

"No, I believe she doesn't. I came into the Reverend's employ when Sophia was fourteen, and I already had an inkling of the strong-willed individual she would become. Sometime after that, I saw how he treated her, his own daughter! I watched from afar, unable to soothe her tears, Mr Grey."

"Pray we get to her in time, Darrowby." There was little else I could do or say.

"Aye, but to which god, Mr Grey?"

"To any and all that will listen. I think we may need all the help that we can muster."

We moved off, descending further into the ziggurat and into the darkness. As we navigated the wide stairwells, we found ourselves subconsciously moving into a line shoulder to shoulder as opposed to the standard line of battle. In a way, the trust, what little there had been between one and another, had been broken. Now, neither of us were willing to show their back to another. Perhaps, out of all of them, Darrowby was one I could count on, but of the Rev and the soldier, I could not trust either of them as far as I could throw them.

From below us, a slow beat of a drum rose to meet us, the tattoo almost melancholic as it bade us to hurry to our deaths. I watched my companions closely as we slowly made our way. Rutherford-Jones clutched the satchel with one hand, the other toying with a large silver crucifix that he had drawn from under his shirt, the ornate cross with the outstretched martyr of the Christian faith attached to a thick silver chain that sat around the older man's neck. His lips moved as they mumbled the words of orisons and prayers to, well, they could have been to any deity.

Darrowby was near to breaking. Beads of perspiration traced their path from his brow and hairline towards his collar, the starch of which was turning a distasteful yellow. Odd, that I remember the little things such as that, an insignificant detail, as clear now decades later as it had been then. Memory over time works mysteriously, a moment of clarity at an opportune moment, or a fog so dense that it clouds everything just a few minutes later.

Only Norton was unmoved, his face set in grim determination, features and attitude as if chiselled by a master such as Michaelangelo. Pistol and blade in hand, he descended the steps as if he were walking through the local woods one Sunday afternoon, bagging game as innocuous as rabbit and fowl. As far removed from the reality as could be, as we were clearly the game here. Prey for God only knew what, or more succinctly, who knew what God was lurking in the tomb below. My father once told me that, a man who is unafraid when staring death and horror in the eyes, is not to be trusted. I have to mention, as a caveat, that he was on his way to the gallows when he told me this, a drunken feud with a fellow farmhand leading to the labourer's murder and my father's execution. Though since that day, I have met many that prove his words true.

The beat of that lone drum lured us deeper into the depths, the staccato of our own heartbeats outpacing it like a racehorse against a mule (or mine, at least – though I suspected that Darrowby's and the Reverend's would be keeping pace with mine). Perversely, each step I took, every stone step I descended, every inch led me closer to my beloved Clara, yet the same took me further away from Boo, who stood a lonely vigil on *The Iceni* above.

We encountered more of the foul dead-but-not-dead that had assailed us in the first chamber. They met the same fate that the first liches had, blown or smashed to dust. Their parched corporeal forms broken and reduced to nothing. I only hope that their twisted and tortured spirits found some rest with their maker. I could not help thinking as we descended further, that our journey was too easy, as if we were being shepherded along a route – like lambs to the slaughter, which would be an appropriate term.

It was some time before we came to another opening, but this room was more antre than chamber, widening out from the foot of the stairs to some sixty feet or more. As it stretched away it front of us, we could define pillars supporting the immense weight above us, as we surely stood in an area that was subterranean. Upon these were bare torches, the flames flickering with an eerie bluish flame. If the chamber had been empty, I was sure that we would have all marvelled at the expansive space that melted away beyond our vision. Alas, empty, it was not.

We were welcomed by the rustling of dessicated skin and linen, aged and dried over years, and the creaking of bones, bleached by time. The dusty figures of a multitude of bodies, long dead and laid to rest, but someone had omitted to tell them of their proper place and their roles to play. Instead, they stood and turned to watch us, empty orbits sensing our movements as if attuned to those guilty of the crime of Life, and who still breathed and respired. Preternaturally, and rather ominously, they made no move against us, merely turning to follow our path. Darrowby circled behind us to ensure they couldn't take us unawares, his shotgun tracking across the arc they formed as we moved on. The continual beat of that infernal drum still assaulted our ears.

Ahead of us, there knelt a figure, facing away from us. They appeared naked, the skin of their back a ghostly white in the dimness of the cavern. Blond hair was pulled up and mounted upon the top of their head, dressed in silver filigree. For want of a better word, their posterior rested upon their bare feet – buttocks that I would have wagered would have belonged to a woman. The whiteness of her skin indicated to me that this was indeed Sophia, my assumption being that, apart from Boo up above, Sophia was the only white woman within a region of a hundred miles, a hypothesis borne out by the way that all three of my companions called out her name simultaneously. The Reverend took a step forward, only to be pulled to a halt by Norton, one hand upon his forearm.

"Hold up one second, Reverend. There's a rum do about this." Norton hissed. I circled as Darrowby had, taking his place as he stared at the focus of his unrequited adoration. My cutlass wavered menacingly towards the undead host, yet they continued to stand still, content to watch us.

Part, the third.
In which Sophia is found, and lost. We dice with Danger and Death.

THE WOMAN STOOD, displaying the fullness of her figure. I was pleased to see the Reverend cross himself and look away, whilst the butler, Darrowby, blushed profusely. I was glad of my self-imposed vigil at the rear of the quartet, sweeping my gaze towards the ones that could strike so quickly. I heard a cry, almost to a man from my companions, and I spun quickly to see what the matter was.

She had turned to face us. I was of no doubt, seeing the consternation upon the Reverend's face, and that of Norton and Darrowby, that this was Sophia. Her appearance was striking, but her face was drawn as if slightly undernourished. A temporary condition that I could see from the brightness of her eyes and the lustre of her straw-coloured hair. What had caused the commotion was not that, nor the nakedness of her figure that she seemed oblivious to and made no movement to cover, but the solid, red circle daubed in what appeared to be blood upon her chest. Judging by the way that rivulets of the sanguine liquid started to trickle between her breasts, the mark was still fresh.

"You should not have come. Father, Mr Norton, Mr Darrowby. You have no business here." She spoke without expression or emotion. As she finished speaking, she seemed to disregard us completely.

"Rubbish, Sophia! Come here now! For once in your life time, please do as I say!" her father exclaimed, breaking free from Norton's grasp and taking a step forward. This movement agitated the waiting undead, their ungodly chatter of noise increasing in volume and intensity. Sophia turned, fire blazing in her eyes as she spat vehemently her response.

"No, father! I will not. There will be no loveless and joyless marriage between myself and," she gave a withering look at Norton, "this charlatan of a man. I am betrothed to Sunat Tow and I will become his bride, and I will live forever as his consort amongst the dark and the night." She stood strong and, for a moment, I was reminded of Boo and the way she channelled her inner strength, the power that is within all women, yet is only visible in a few due to the patriarchal society that we have created along with its rules and laws. She exerted such forceful demeanour that, if *The Iceni* had not been entrapped by the supernatural auroras above, I would have left there and then. Then, for a mere moment, it appeared as if she had been replaced with, I assume, the original Sophia.

Her features softened and the blaze that flamed within her eyes were quenched with a look of terror and despair. She reached out a hand, imploring us, as she begged for assistance.

"James! Help me, please. He plans to take me." She looked about her furtively, and then back to the four of us. And, as immediately as the old Sophia had broken free of the internal gaol that this Sunat Tow had ensnared her in, the gates slammed back shut on her, returning her to the emotionless state she had first appeared in. Sophia raised her arms until they were perpendicular to her torso, reminiscent of Da Vinci's Vitruvian Man. The assembled horde of animated corpses fell silent along with the ever-present drumbeat. She exclaimed loudly, announcing the arrival of her groom-to-be.

"Behold, Sunat Tow the magnificent, Master of this Necropolis, Devourer of Flesh and Souls, Giver of Life-in-Death."

A flame burst into life before her, taking form on the damp stone. It grew in stature and gyrated, slowly at first, then with sweeping intensity. Dancing as if in some lunatic, frenzied reel, it circled madly, spawning smaller flames behind it, tracing a circle across the stone. Amplifying in strength and size, every colour and hue of yellow, orange and red blended before our eyes. We all took a step backwards as the heat increased, searing the skin of our faces.

A figure appeared within the circle. As the fire subsided, we were blessed, or cursed, with our first sight of Sophia's groom-to-be. It stood taller than Norton by at least two feet. A dark cowl covered his face and shoulders, and material of the same fabric was wrapped about his waist in the style of the indigenous people above. Whilst his subjects were little more than bleached bone and dried gristle, the necromancer of the island had some, albeit wiry and parched, flesh upon his bones. The skin, stretched tightly across this framework, was pallid and grey, the mottled purple grey so favoured by Varley in his Dutch works. Across his chest, the black outline of a skull had been carved into the dead flesh.

His fingers ended with what only could be described as talons or claws, the nails black with time and grime, the edges chipped and cracked. About his neck was draped a heavy chain, the iron links rusted over the years. The chain was looped loosely over his shoulders and neck, with each end connected to a cage, similarly constructed cage of corroded metal, about the size of a man's head. A pulsing blue gem filled each cage, but instead of hanging from the chain, the gems floated in the air to the side of his head. It was as if the primary function of the chain and cages were to ensnare the gems and keep them tethered to the lich, least they float away.

"You are guilty of the crime of Life. When I have taken Sophia to become Sunat Ta'Tow-ken, then I will pronounce sentence upon you all, and you will kneel and pledge your fealty to your overlord, as my many vassals have done." He waved an arm to indicate the still silent and immobile undead.

"But Sophia still lives..." started Norton, who brought the

rest of the sentence to an abrupt stop, realising what Sunat Tow had in store for his betrothed.

"No!" the cry from Darrowby was loud and wild, the cry of a man who was want to lay his life down for the sake of the one he loved. As would I have done if Clara was stood where Sophia now stood. Norton holstered his pistol and in one fluid movement unslung his rifle from his shoulder. He wrapped the long strap about his hand several times, taking up the slack, and pulled the heavy brass-shod butt into his shoulder. As he peered down the sights, Sunat Tow laughed. A deep laugh that resonated through us all. The undead chittered, the noise rising to a crescendo as they fed from the sound of their liege.

The noise in the chamber was nothing in comparison to the cannon-like retort of Norton's rifle. At the sound all fell silent except for Rutherford-Jones who held aloft his crucifix and spoke clearly and loudly, though not as loudly as the mountain cracking sound of Norton's Enfield Treble 8.

"And the seventh angel poured out his vial into the air; and there came a Great Voice out of the Temple of Heaven, from the throne, saying, It is done. And there were voices, and thunders, and lightnings; and there was a great earthquake, such as was not since men were upon the Earth, so mighty an earthquake, and so great."

There was a whirring sound from Norton's rifle, as the mechanical elements inside pulled and pushed the shell casing, ejecting it from the top of the gun. The shiny brass casing, four inches in length and a bore of a full inch, clattered on the stone flags. There was a low click as the clip moved one space upwards, filling the chamber of the Treble 8 with another shell of destruction. Norton lowered the rifle to inspect his handiwork.

His aim had been true, that much I can say. Even now, so many years later, I can categorically state that he had not missed. The evidence was before my eyes. A hole, larger than my clenched fist, had been punched through the undead Lord's chest. It sat square between the eyes of the skull tattoo carved upon his grey skin. I saw the flames of the torches behind flicker through the cavity. Smoke curled from the barrel of Norton's rifle and also from the edge of the hideous wound, and the acrid stench of cordite hung in the air.

Sunat Tow stood still, the mystical gems faltering slightly as they tried to escape from his clutches. His head bowed slightly, as if the faceless void was inspecting the wound that would lead to his second death. He laughed again, and I watched as the hole slowly closed up. Where once had sat a wound that would have felled a charging bull elephant, there was nary a mark upon the chest of the demon. I blanched. Norton stared for a second, then brought the rifle back to his shoulder once again.

Then, to put not a fine point upon it, there came a hollering as if the banshees and demons of every plane of Hell had been unchained and unleashed upon the world. The undead took umbrage at the attack upon their lord, either that or some unspoken command had been passed between liege and fealtor. They rushed forward, faster than the ambling beasts that had attacked us previously. Perhaps, in close proximity to that of Sunat Tow, their power and strength was increased.

We formed a square, a defensive arrangement of the smallest perimeter and defended ourselves at great cost to the enemy. Even the Reverend struck out with a blade, his crucifix in his other hand. I heard the boom of Darrowby's scattergun, the 8-bore shells wreaking havoc among the attackers. I took down several with my pistol, each shot easily finding the forehead of an undead at such close range. Snapping my pistol back into its holster, I switched the heavy cutlass to my right hand, freeing the mechanical fist of my left to act as both weapon and shield. Norton, likewise, dealt death and destruction with machete and pistol, the Treble 8 no weapon for a close melee.

I watched Sunat Tow beckon Sophia towards him, as I cleaved my blade through more parched and dehydrated corpses. She took his outstretched hand and rose of the ground, her feet at least a yard clear from the floor. The giant lich bade her lay back with a movement of his free hand, her body following his silent commands. She levitated, like some damn Indian fakir, face up and almost limp. His hand came down towards her bare chest, the talons scraping over the red circle crudely daubed upon the milky-whiteness of her skin. A rush of realisation flooded into my synapses. This was how he intended to take her as his bride.

"No, no, no!" I yelled, swiping in a wide arc ahead of me. I had gained some space to draw my Lee Enfield and reload it with a clip from my waistcoat bandolier. I fumbled the loading, as my cutlass dangled from its wrist strap. As I snapped the clip into place and thumber the hammer back, I saw Sunat's claw-like talons push into Sophia's chest. To my incredulous amazement, there was no sudden eruption of blood from the wound, no gore, no flood of blood or sanguinity. Neither did the ribcage offer any hindrance to the penetration of his hand.

I felled another opponent, my mechanical hand crushing their head in a billow of dust, as I raised the Lee Enfield. I fired the entire clip, the bullets heading straight towards the demonic figure who taunted us with his very presence upon this earth. One bullet disappeared into the void that was his cowl, most of the others struck true, puncturing the chest of Sunat Tow. I expected the same result as Norton's shell, and, alas, wasn't disappointed. The last bullet ricocheted from the cage of one of the floating gems, striking another opponent. The gem and its cage jerked quickly, disappearing behind the lich lord.

Sunat's hand clenched about something deep in Sophia's chest and the still figure spasmed into movement. A soft moan fell from her lips as her suitor twisted his hand and withdrew it.

In his fist, the beast held Sophia's beating heart, blood now dripping from the eviscerated organ, and pumping from the ruptured valves, yet there was no wound upon her chest itself. Sophia's chest rose, her back arching and then she fell still. All four of us exclaimed at once her name.

I let of a flurry of shots, and heard Norton do the same. Sunat Tow had the audacity to be unaffected by any of our shots. Darrowby had reached the point where reloading was not an option, and had reversed his shot gun, gripped the barrel and applied agricultural hews with the stock that would make any gentleman playing at Lords or the Oval wince. The air hung thick with the stench of cordite and the dust of battered corpses, yet we were like Cnut, king of the North Sea Empire, attempting to turn the tide.

"Grey!" Norton shouted above the clamour of battle, waving his machete towards where Sunat Tow towered over the still body of Sophia, suspended haplessly in the air before him. The giant raised his arms towards the heavens, far above, and threw his head back. Black smoke poured from within his hood, forming tendrils that writhed and snaked their way towards Sophia. I watched, struck dumb at a terrifying sight. The smoke curled around Sophia, twisting and turning about the prone figure, arching above her face before plunging down. It was as if they were probing her, endeavouring to seek out the entrances to her body. Succeed they did, seeping into her mouth, nostrils and ears.

Her body danced and convulsed as if she was stricken with that strange curse known as St Vitus' Dance, her limbs twisting and turning in unnatural patterns. I felt someone stumble against me and clutch at my arm, and looked down to see Rutherford-Jones' hand upon me. A look of terror was etched into his face as Sunat Tow's essence poured into the dead body of his daughter. Darrowby howled in anguish as he watched the love of his eye tortured in death, and even the spurned Norton swore and cursed as only a soldier could, raising his pistol to fire several rounds into the hooded void that was the lich's face. Once again, the caged crystals ducked and bobbed behind the lich.

The minions of Sunat Tow, undeterred by the carnage that we had dealt to their ranks, renewed their efforts, pressing us together until our shoulders were touching. The Reverend collapsed shrieking to the ground, two undead upon him. Darrowby crashed the butt of his shotgun against one, smashing it to dust. My metal hand closed upon the other, snapping the neck like a dry twig underfoot, and I pulled the (re)newed corpse away. A torrent of blood poured from a wound on the Reverend's throat, and he desperately clasped his hand over it. It is often at the strangest and inappropriate times that a thought comes to you – as I watched the Reverend vainly try to stem the flow, I was reminded of the little Dutch boy plugging the hole in the dike to save Holland. I felt the press of bodies against me and I prayed. I am not afraid to say that, even now so many years after. I prayed to any god that would listen, even to Reverend Rutherford-Jones' god, that had so cruelly punished him for his deviances.

My prayers, and also those of my compatriots I would assume, were answered, by God working in mysterious ways. God, whether it was Rutherford-Jones' god, or any one of the countless thousands that man has prayed to since those first days that we huddled around fires in caves, sent retribution in the form of Boo toting a pair of Webley & Scott Double Nines. She stormed in, the muzzle flashes from the pistols lighting up the chamber.

Worried about what was happening within the ziggurat, Boo had left her post to be my saviour once again. Desertion of one's post in Her Majesty's Airship Corps, or even under the ensign of privateers such as Captain Harriman would lead to a quick jig from the yardarm, however I made a note to only thank my erstwhile companion from the bottom of my heart.

The fury of her assault as she entered the chamber behind us would not be forgotten by Darrowby, Norton and myself for as long as we live. It was something that I have become accustomed to many times since. The hordes about us were blasted into oblivion, releasing whatever spirit or life force – should you believe in such things – had been encased within the dehydrated husks. With breathing room, literal breathing room, we took stock of our situation.

"Abelard." She pushed up the brow of her hat with the muzzle of a pistol.

"Boo." I nodded in appreciation and thanks.

She looked down at the Reverend, his hand pressed against his neck, a carmine flood pouring from between his fingers. A gamut of emotions crossed her face as she witnessed the final struggles of her nemesis. His free hand scrambled to his satchel, pulling the Circlet of Mahakali from within. Ignoring the heat from the mystical band, he raised it towards his own forehead, his hand shaking every inch of the way. The rubies flickered in the torchlight, the scarlet hue matching the blood on his other hand.

"No, you don't!" Darrowby exclaimed, grasping the Reverend's wrist. In his dying throes, the older man thrashed about, forcing Darrowby to lose his grip.

"Help me, Grey!" Darrowby struck the Reverend with his fist. "He means to use that on himself, whilst his daughter lies in the grasp of that beast! He has run his life, whilst Sophia has barely started hers."

"What is that thing?" asked Boo, rapidly loading a new clip into each of her pistols. I realised that in standing guard above, she had missed the revelation of the circlet and Rutherford-Jones' betrayal of his own god.

"Time is of the essence, Boo!" I shouted as I knelt, grabbing the old man's arm. "Just keep those infernal things at bay." I glanced at the approaching ranks of shambling husks.

"Aye-aye, Capt'n." she laughed, and the cavern shook once again with the sound of the Double Nines. I heard the locking of Darrowby's shotgun and was shocked to see him aim at the old man.

"Darrowby, no!" I called out. "His life is not worth the burden on your soul!" I continued to struggle against the arm of Rutherford-Jones. It is often said that some men, when faced with their impending death, find an inner strength unbeknownst to them. Rutherford-Jones was one such man, and I found myself struggling against herculean strength.

"I cannot stand by and watch this liar and coward extend his own life, whilst Sophia writhes in that demon's hands! Not when that gem can save her."

"She's dead, you fool!" hissed the Reverend through gritted teeth, blood and spittle spraying from his lips.

I had stood next to artillery and cannons when they have been fired, and the noise of the shot was as deafening and striking as being below decks in an air or sea battle. My head rang, and I looked up at Darrowby. His face showed a look of shock, yet no smoke curled from the end of the barrel of his shot gun. The smell of cordite came from my right, where Norton stood. The long-barrelled pistol pointed directly at the mess that had once been a man's head. Norton, his blond hair tussled with sweat and the grime of the battle, locked his eyes with mine for a brief second.

"When you have a mad dog, Grey, you put the cur down." He reloaded, then fired again, this time towards the undead that Boo was keeping at bay. "Darrowby, your time is now. Make your choice." With that he entered the fray, pistol blazing and machete hacking.

"Darrowby?" I enquired of the man who stood rooted to the spot. He looked at me, then his former employer (what remained of him), and then to the circlet. He snatched it with one hand, the heat causing him to flinch somewhat.

"Your assistance, Mr Grey, would be appreciated."

"Come then," I answered, grabbing my cutlass and pistol. Together we charged for Sunat Tow and the stricken Sophia. The black mist still poured from his voluminous hood, streaming towards Sophia. Her features had become twisted, the skin pulling tight across her bones beneath. A black mass writhed over her chest, a vivid reminder of the fatal blow that Sunat Tow had dealt her.

I wondered at the idiocy of Darrowby's plan. We had all seen her heart, that organ of life, pulled from within her chest. In love, one would do anything to save the object of your desire – and as Norton had put it, this was Darrowby's time.

My sword came flashing down on the demon that was Sunat Tow, and the blade passed through his torso, the wounded skin closing up behind the blade's journey. Darrowby, likewise, unleashed both barrels of his shotgun at point black range. This at least caused the foulness to recoil slightly, and I took heart, firing my own pistol at the beast. Sunat Tow struck out, his talon like hand aiming directly for my chest.

I dropped my cutlass, the blade hanging loosely from its wrist cord and my metallic hand clasped about the fist of the demon. I knew my very life depended upon whether I could hold his claw at bay. For a centuries old corpse, Sunat Tow was surprisingly strong. My upper arm was tight against my chest, my elbow perpendicular to the same. My muscles were taut, straining against the power of the lich Lord. Horrified, I watched as his finger extended, elongating to an unnatural length. It sought its path between the small girders, for want of a better word, that made my hand what it is. It inched towards my heart and I could feel a coldness about me.

"Darrowby, are you done?" I called out, mesmerized by the approaching finger.

"Nearly, Mister Grey." replied the butler.

I looked up, my eyes drawn towards the darkness within the folds of Sunat Tow's hood. I could have been looking into an abyss for all that I saw. And then, a revelation came to me. The strange gems encased within the iron cages, connected to Sunat Tow by way of those heavy chains. The way they moved, dodging behind his body as shots were fired towards them. Could they be the source of his power?

"Boo, Norton! Shoot the gems, destroy both of them!"

His nail reached my waistcoat and passed through the heavy cotton material. I felt the stab of ice pierce my skin and a chill spread through my veins. The beating of my heart, that should have been akin to that of a racehorse, slowed indeterminably. My arm trembled, energy seeping from my muscles.

I wondered if Boo or Norton had heard me and made to repeat myself. My mouth was dry, my tongue falling over the words, and I looked down. Sunat Tow's finger was sunk up to the first knuckle into my chest. My head swam, and I noticed the shadowy form of Darrowby clutching the naked Sophia to his chest. As I blacked out, my ears rang with the sound of the world exploding.

Part, the fourth.
Aftermath, in which a final betrayal is uncovered, love reaches beyond the strangest of boundaries, and a bond is formed.

I CAME to a few minutes later, or so I was told. Of Sunat Tow and his horde, there was naught to see, save for the few lengths of heavy iron chain, with empty cages attached to their ends. My head pounded with pain and my chest felt stiff. In fact, it would be several days before I could breathe properly.

"You had me worried, Abelard, especially when you collapsed. I thought that demon had taken you." Boo gushed as she raised a flask to my lips, the strong port filling my mouth with warmth. She dropped her eyes, and blushed slightly.

"The gems? I take it that worked? I must thank you for saving me once again."

"Norton had a hand in it also, Abelard. He was the one that shot the second gem. Once I had taken the first, the remaining one ducked and dived like something possessed. Which I suppose it was."

"Yes, Grey. You were right." Norton interrupted any further response from Boo as he stood above me, resting the butt of his hunting rifle on the stone floor. I looked across to the body of Reverend Rutherford-Jones, pushing myself up from the floor to try to stand. My head swam and my stomach churned.

"I have already looked, Abelard." Boo's tone and face fell.

"And?" I asked, knowing the answer before Boo's words fell upon my ears.

"There is nothing there, Abelard. He lied." He had written no letters of commendation, no testimonials to the fact that I had helped him in his quest to rescue Sophia. As crestfallen as I was – without a letter from Rutherford-Jones, I could not return to England to see my Clara again. Deep down though, I was not surprised. If the shoe had been on the other foot, I suppose I would have done the same. Maybe he always intended to write them once Sophia had been rescued and repatriated. Maybe he didn't. Of that, I will never know. I hoped, though it mattered not in the grand scheme of things, that he would have kept his word.

"No need to worry, Grey. I will write to my father once I am back in Darwin. You kept your word, unlike others. We may not see eye to eye, but we are alike, you and I. And, I suppose, I owe you and Boo, my life." Norton spoke again.

"I owe you mine, Norton. As do we all."

"I'll explain Rutherford-Jones as a casualty of war. He will not be missed in the avenues of power in London."

At the mention of the Reverend, I was reminded of the reason that we had come to las Isla de los Muertos.

"Sophia?" I sat up and looked about. Darrowby stepped from behind me, and that day, in the Temple of Sunat Tow, I witnessed a miracle. One of many in my lifetime, I might add. Darrowby held Sophia's hand and she, rather awkwardly, stood. Boo's frock coat masked most of her nakedness, covering to her thighs, leaving her bare lower legs on display, milk white in the torch light. I averted my eyes, and focused on her face.

At that moment, there seemed to be little left of the woman that I had caught such a fleeting glimpse of when we had first encountered her. Her eyes were sunken and shut, the dark pits surmounted and countered by the brightness of the golden band that sat upon her forehead. The gems glowed like a thousand flames, a fire that mirrored the spirit that was once present.

Oh, how I was wrong. With a snap, she opened her eyes and I was met with the radiance of sapphires, the blue of her irises like that of a summer day's sky. Deep within, I could see and sense her countenance had not been destroyed by the demon that had subverted her. Finally, I could see why my companions had, at one time or another, been besotted with her. When she spoke, her voice was stilted and slow, but had a musical quality.

"I must thank you for your efforts to save me, and for the second life that you have all given to me." She looked upwards, to the cavernous roof of the chamber. "The mystical field that has held your ship has gone, sent to oblivion alongside Sunat Tow. You will be able to leave now."

I turned to Darrowby.

"Darrowby, you are more than welcome to accompany us, once we reach civilisation. You've proven yourself today. I have a feeling that you would be a great asset to *The Iceni*. That is, if you are in agreement, Boo?"

"Of course!"

My legs trembled with the exertion of standing, and Boo came to my aid as she answered. I felt the warmth of her body as she clasped me close, propping me up. Norton shouldered his rifle.

"She is right, we should be away. Who knows what else inhabits this cursed place," he announced.

His former lover turned to him. She raised an arm and the normally fearless soldier shrank away. I could not tell whether it was through fear or with disgust.

"You need not worry, Mr Norton. Nothing inhabits this place save for you, and the beasts that crawl and slither. The spirits of the dead have gone with Sunat Tow. As I would have gone, were it not for this circlet."

"Still, we should be away. Let us leave the dead with their new Mistress. I must return to my regiment with great haste."

"No!" Darrowby exclaimed, stepping forward between Sophia and Norton. He turned, taking Sophia's hands in his. "We came here to return you home. You should come with us. I thought I had lost you twice, first to Mr Norton, and thence to Sunat Tow. Please, I beg of you, allow me to have some purpose in life, beyond that of serving the undeserving."

"You are quite mad, Darrowby. Of that, I am certain." Norton tutted with a sneer. I must confess, in the moment, I thought the same.

"Please, Sophia." Darrowby implored.

Sophia stood stock still. Her chest neither rose or fell, the need for breath long gone. Her eyes dulled slightly, but then blazed again, as the crooked cross upon the lozenge that sat centre of her forehead did the same.

"Mr Grey" She addressed me, almost without looking at me. "If you would allow it, I would be grateful to accompany you upon your return. There is nothing here for me." She kept her eyes on Darrowby, the gems on the diadem brighter with each word. "And out there, there is everything for me. Especially if you are there to share them with me, James."

With a look of shock on his face, James Darrowby clamoured to say something, turning redder than the proverbial beetroot as he did so. When she had addressed her plea to 'James' that Sunat Tow intended to take her, she had not been referring to James Norton but to Darrowby.

"James. It has always been you. I saw how you acted around me when you first came into Father's employ, and especially so when I attained womanhood. My strength, my drive to push myself to do the best that I could, came as much from your love and attention that you gave, as it did with the hatred I had for my father.

"If only the world could accept love and kinship between the echelons of society, then it would be a better place." She continued. Darrowby looked across to me, and then to Boo. It was my erstwhile companion who broke first, laughing and cheering.

"It looks like *The Iceni* has doubled her crew!"

I nodded, then grabbed Darrowby's hand and shook it as only a man could, a firm grip and minimal movement. I wondered what adventures lay ahead for the four of us; four outcasts in a world of danger and demons, monsters and magic. I wondered where we would go from here, and if any further companions should join us.

"You are all mad, indeed. Stark, raving mad!" Norton muttered and started the long climb up to the surface.

Tales from the Dell

Our other great love at Chez Northwood, on top of working, horses and dogs, music, and TV, is playing board games. Not your old version of Monopoly, or Rummi-Cub, but modern Euro Games.

One of the first we purchased was Everdell, a delightful game where you create a city using cards representing either buildings and characters (or critters – as the cities are populated by such bizarre creatures such as Ferry Ferrets, Barge Toads, and Farmer mice!). One of the first, but also an all-time favourite game of ours, it gave rise to a new world and a fresh hero to write of – Javen Silvertail.

9

The Triple Death
In which, a traitor is named, and a critter flees.

Griswold the barge toad sat at his usual booth in the corner of the Rotten Acorn. A hard day's work on the fast-running brook had left him aching. He was getting old, proven by the fact he ached more than yesterday, and yesterday he ached more than the day before. But now he could relax, his webbed fingers wrapped around the waxed leaf tankard. The dark ale looked inviting, it smelled inviting, and if this batch of Old Brock's ale was like his last one, (and why wouldn't it be? The old badger had been brewing in the dell as long as anyone could remember) then the taste would be like moonlight streaming through the canopy of the oaks that littered the dell.

He looked through the small window across the bar. The sky was the shade of mulberry and orange, that wondrous hue announcing fair weather in the morn. Perhaps there was only an hour or so of daylight left. Time to enjoy the ale he had earned before hopping back down to the bank of the brook and back to his wife. Raising the tankard towards his mouth, he closed his eyes and inhaled the subtle aromas.

The crash of the door jarred him from his reverie, causing him to slop ale over his fingers. The room hushed as the occupants all turned to stare at the newcomers. Three rats strode in, each carrying a spear which leant a further degree of menace to their demeanour and swagger. The dark blue caps they wore announced to all that they were members of the Rat Guard, bodyguard and soldiers of Mariuz II, King of the Dell. Their noses twitched as the made their way towards the bar. A path seemed to melt as the critters of the dell shrank aside. No-one in their right mind messed with the King's Guard. A starling walked with them; a satchel worn close to the iridescent feathers of his chest, a sword at his hip that made his gait even more awkward.

Griswold recognized him, as did many of the customers of the Rotten Acorn. Samel, the king's Chancellor. His piercing eyes scanned the room before settling upon Old Brock, the bar badger. He squawked, causing the old badger to jump.

"Your attention is mandatory!" As if to accentuate his staccato address, one of the rat guards stepped across the doorway, just in time to bar the path of a couple of mice, eager to withdraw from the proceedings. The appearance of the rat guards and Chancellor Samel meant trouble for someone.

The chancellor rooted through his satchel with his yellow beak, producing a roll of paper. He shook it towards one of the guards, who took it and unrolled it. The guard drew a small hammer and four nails from his own pouch and proceeded to nail the scroll to the board that stood upon the bar proclaiming Old Brock's wares and prices. With just one blow each, the four nails were driven into the old wood of the sign. From where Griswold sat, he could make out the headline scrawl. 'Exiled!' A sketch of a rat sat underneath, one eye blackened and bruised. The ears were torn and bloody.

"In the name of Mariuz II, King of the Dell, Lord of all Rats and Critters, Baron of the Beasts, let it be known to all citizens of the Dell that a traitor has been uncovered, here in our sacred and peaceful land." Samel paused whilst the inside of the Rotten Acorn filled with an increasing murmur of astonishment. Whilst many of the clientele of Brock's bar cared little for the chancellor, the mere mention of a traitor had certainly piqued their interest. As it was with any community, sensational sleaze caught the ear and tempted the attention. The starling felt the eyes of the entire bar upon him as he continued with his delivery.

"A member of the Rat Guard, once a loyal servant of the king, has been found guilty of treason against His Majesty. The dirty traitor has been subjected to the sentence of the Triple Death!" Griswold sucked his breath in, the Triple Death indeed. Not since his early years and the tales told by his grandfather, had he heard of a critter being subjected to such ignominy. The punishment hadn't been levied in the reign of Mariuz's father, or his grandfather, yet the new king was intent on ruling with a rod of iron. The Triple Death; Shredding, Exiled and Outlawed, with a price on upon the unfortunate criminal's head. The toad saw a few younger critters look blankly at the proclamation.

"It is hereby proclaimed that Javen Silvertail," Samel paused again, knowing full well the effect the name would have on the occupants of the bar. He waited for the simmering to die down. How the mighty had fallen, he thought as he smiled to himself and witnessed the confusion and astonishment within. That's right, he thought. The one-time favourite of King Memfraz, Mariuz's father, was a traitor. The saviour of the resin mines, the dog-killer and many more feats of heroism would be talked about no more, all overshadowed by the darkest crime of all. Treason.

"That's right! Javen Silvertail has been Shredded. Javen Silvertail has been exiled upon pain of death should he ever return to the Dell. Javen Silvertail is now outlaw, with a price of five silver crowns upon his head. Anyone found harbouring the criminal will be subjected to Shredding." Griswold felt many within the small bar wince. Shredding involved the ears of the guilty being torn to shreds, marking the unfortunate for the rest of their life.

"What did he do?" the old voice of Brock crackled into life.

"Treason. Is that not enough! Is the word of your king not enough?"

"Of course..." stammered the old badger.

"But what exactly did he do?" echoed Dam the Bard, the old beaver who sat next to the fire in the corner of the bar. Some thought the old bard mad, yet all agreed that he could sing, and keep, a tune. "The rat who stood against a dog and won. The rat who saved many when the banks of the brook broke and flooded Berrytown. What wrong did he do?" The tone was mocking with a hint of confrontation layered within the words. It was obvious to Chancellor Samel where the bard's allegiance lay.

"Very well." Samel paused and stared first at Dam, and then various others in the crowded room. Only Dam the Bard met and kept his gaze. "Several hours ago, the Rat Guard were called to a warehouse on the lake side. Word had been given that members of the Red Paw were meeting, plotting the downfall and murder of His Majesty, King Mariuz II." His dramatic address fell flat as a hedgehog near to Dam the Bard collapsed in giggles. He yelped as one of the blue capped rats jabbed him with the butt of their spear.

"Enough!" Shouted the starling, his voice rising above the

murmur that threatened to claim the room. "Your hero, Silvertail, was a member of that cell. Then when our brave rats assaulted the building, he not only claimed the life of one of his old comrades, but he also slew his new compatriots in a cowardly act." His wings fluttered slightly as he listened to the sharp intakes of breath from the clientele. They didn't want to believe it, not of the hero of the dell. He waited to deliver the coup-de-grace.

"And then, in one final, failed attempt to escape the blades of justice, your flawed hero found himself in the path of Fisherwoman Boort. The blackhearted knave cut her down without a second thought." There was a sharp intake of breath from the four corners of the room. Fisherwoman Boort was well known throughout the Dell, well known and well loved. The Chancellor continued, pointing to the poster on the bar board. "That is your hero! That is the traitor, Javen Silvertail. He was taken prisoner shortly afterwards, and Mariuz the Merciful took pity on him."

"By giving him the Triple Death?" Dam the Bard thumped the floor with the flat of his tail. "It would have been kinder to have killed him outright."

Chancellor Samel nodded, trying to look thoughtful.

"Who dare question the words and thoughts of a king?" It wasn't a threat or accusation but a rhetorical question. Who indeed? He though. The Triple Death, a punishment for the most heinous of crimes. The pain of the Shredding came first. That act this evening had been carried out by Mariuz's chief bodyguard, the weasel myrmidon, Art Sevrance. Fierce, unyielding and slightly psychotic, the weasel was the better of any critter in the Dell when it came to fighting, with either sword or claw.

He thought back and shuddered at the memory of the flashing claws and teeth, and the spray of blood that splashed from the thin membranous ears of the fallen hero. Most of all, though, he remembered the pain etched onto the rat's face and the pitiful cries that had finally escaped from between the teeth of Javen's clamped jaw.

After the pain would come the Humiliation of the Exile. Forsaken by friends and family, shunned by all, the torn ears a traumatic branding of a heart most foul. Alone and banished from the community of the Dell, myths told of those of old who had suffered the Triple Death. Many had succumbed to the depths of blackness and madness, as the feeling of solitude worked its deadly blade into their very psyche.

Finally, Outlaw; the true meaning of the word. The traitor was removed from the protective shield of Justice and Law. Any act could be done unto the outlaw, and it would be justified in the eyes of the law. Unruly youths could throw stones to force them on their way, and their goods and riches could be stolen with impunity. Nothing could help the reputation, not to mention the purse, of a young sword more than returning home to the Dell with the head of an outlaw on a stick.

"Let the King's word be done." Samel smiled. The upstart would be well on his way beyond the borders of the Dell by now, that is, if he had any sense. He made his way from the hushed crowd, his accompanying guards covering his path and ushered others out of the way.

Griswold bent to sup his pint. Now, there was a turn up for the books, he thought. Old Silvertail a traitor. Could it really be? When the voice spoke, it came from behind Griswold, further back in the booth that had been empty when he had first sat down. The words were quiet but were announced clearly with a tinge of pain bleeding between them.

"It was not like that."

Griswold jumped as if the old barge hand had sat upon a thistle. He managed to quell any sound though a few suds of ale again splashed from his tankard.

"He lies."

He looked across the bar as the chancellor and his guards

stood by the doorway, about to hammer another poster to the door itself. Griswald knew the voice, he knew whose words lingered in the smoke laden air of Old Brock's Bar. He knew without looking who sat next to him. Something deep within his heart forced him to stay silent, overriding the urging of his brain to cry out in alarm.

He glanced sideways. The figure was shrouded in the folds of a dark cloak, formed more from patches than the original material. Griswold could just make out the whiskers and a grey snout poking out from within. The soft grey fur was flecked with still wet blood.

"It was not like that. He lies." The figure repeated his words, speaking so softly that Griswold's beating heart nearly drowned them out. The barge toad raised his tankard to his mouth, more to disguise his words than to drink.

"Give me one good reason not to call out right now."

"Because you know it's not true. Deep down, you do."

"Try me." He growled, trying to sound unimpressed, but the rat spoke the truth. He doubted many in Brock's Bar believed the account told by the starling. There had to be more to it than that. The cloaked figure sat back, shrinking into the corner of the booth. He all but disappeared into the shadow cast by the lantern that hung from the ceiling over the neighbouring booth. Finally, he spoke.

"I had retired to my cell after evening repast, my duty done for the day, or so I thought. There came a knock at my door. It was the sergeant calling me to arms. A warning of a Red Paw cell had been raised and Albrus Longsnout had called for reinforcements. I quickly armed and made my way down past the bramble fields to the lake. It was there that I met Fisherwoman Boort."

He raised a hand to rub the end of his snout. Griswold couldn't help but notice the battered fingers on the hand of the rat.

"I swear as the brook runs fast and deep, that I left Otter Boort alive and well. Though the news she gave me disturbed me somewhat, and I hurried along the path to Albrus." He turned towards the barge toad so that Griswold could see his eyes, bright within the hood.

"She told me that it was not a Red Paw cell, just some youths from Elderwood meeting and passing time. True, they had no time for Mariuz." As Javen mentioned the king's name, Griswold grunted as if to agree and say who did. "The only thing they were plotting was finding some bramble wine and possibly scrumping from Old Dan's orchard. She wanted to tell Albrus that the youths weren't armed, and that they weren't terrorists. One of them was the son of her neighbour. A good lad.

"So, I hurried along and caught Albrus and his squad near the warehouse. Just in time, or so I thought, as they were about to storm the building. When I told him what Otter Boort had said, he believed me not. I begged and begged for a chance to talk to the youths but to no avail. It was then the weasel appeared, something thrown over his shoulder." The rat shuddered as an uncomfortable memory flooded his mind. Griswold could hear the tempo of the words slow down.

"I finally recognised the dress, that purple that Boort favoured. My heart was in my mouth as Art asked me which way I had approached from. When I replied 'from the bramble fields', I could see the wry smile he gave Albrus as he dumped his burden on the ground before us. 'Did you run into Fisherwoman Boort?' he asked me. It was all I could do to stammer out an answer as I looked down upon her broken and bloodied body. I didn't think I had to announce my innocence either. That is, until they both accused me of murdering poor Boort! I have no time for that weasel, but Albrus enlisted in the Rat Guard in the same four-season as I did. We were barrack mates for many a season. I couldn't believe that he would be taken in by such falsehood."

Griswold drained his tankard and contemplated getting another. He thought better of it, unwilling to call attention to Javen whilst he was talking, but also not trusting himself to give the fugitive away, either consciously or subconsciously.

"They grabbed me and took Thorn." Javen mentioned the sword that was almost as famous as he was. Infamous now, Griswold corrected himself. The rat continued. "Then Albrus passed judgement in Mariuz's name and then the weasel did this." He raised his hands to the hood, ready to show the old barge toad the Shredding.

"No. I do not need to see it." He shook his head and looked furtively about the room. "Besides, someone might see you. And then we are both in trouble."

Javen Silvertail reflected on the toad's words. Slowly his hands lowered to his lap. Griswold spoke again.

"So old Fatty Mariuz didn't pass judgement on you himself?"

"He wasn't there, but he knew. It was always his plan. After all, he hadn't forgotten that I had apparently insulted him at his coronation, when I heaped praise on his father, Memfraz, for being a great king – and then said nothing about him." He paused and rubbed his snout again. "But if you feel insulted if someone tells the truth, then maybe you need to listen carefully."

"Oh, it seemed he listened. And remembered." Griswold grimaced. Where Javen had started to push his hood back, his grey nose now poked out further. A solitary speck of blood had formed upon a whisker, weighing the hair down as it edged towards the point. Any second now, it would plummet to the table below.

"And the youngsters? Samel said that you brought them down as well."

"No, Albrus's rats led them out, bound and blindfolded. They are already in the mines, Griswold. They won't see the sun set on the Dell again." He paused, thinking of the youngsters. The mines beyond Briar Hill were reserved for only the worst criminals in the Dell. Find yourself there, and you never came out. "Both you and I know, if I had killed them as the starling said, I would have done them a great service. Something is rotten here in the Dell, Griswold. Rotten and stinking."

"We all think that, old friend." The barge toad gulped at his words. He hadn't thought about Javen as a friend before, but it was true. Javen was well liked by many of the Dell's critters. It was just that no one called him 'friend'. Now he had, turning himself into an accomplice of the so-called traitor.

"But I must leave now, it isn't safe for me here. Just get by as best you can until I can find out what is afoot and return."

"Then why have you come here? If it were me, I would be halfway to Salthaven by now. And past it by morning."

"I need Thorn. She was my father's sword and his father's sword, and before that, his father's. For one hundred four-seasons Thorn has been a blade for a Silvertail, no-one else. I cannot allow her to fall into infamy and ill repute in the hands of Albrus or the king." He paused and shuddered again. "Or that weasel."

"You are quite mad."

"Yes. I suppose I am. Mad at having put up with Mariuz and his paranoia for the last four-season, that is. I should have retired when Memfraz passed away."

"Who would have looked over the critters in the Dell, then?"

The rat fell silent, unable to answer the barge toad's question. Finally, he stood. Griswold pushed out an arm, pulling him back down in his seat.

"What are you doing?" he hissed.

"I need to go."

"Yes, but not out of the front door. Samel has only just left. He could be waiting."

"He thinks I am, as you say, halfway to Salthaven."

"And Albrus?"

Javen paused. Then clenched his fists in frustration.

"No, he knows I will come for Thorn. He will be outside."

"Then do the unexpected. Leave through the window. Go, and leave Thorn for now. You think of it as an extension of your family, but in truth, it is but a blade. There are hundred, thousands more blades under the sun."

Javen chuckled.

"Why not do both? Now, that will be very unexpected."

The barge toad looked confused. The rat leant in conspiratorially and whispered.

"This is what I need you to do."

ALBRUS LONGSNOUT PULLED his cloak about him a little tighter than he liked. At his age, he should be back in the nest, curled up with a flagon of ale. You knew you were old when the flagons of berry ale appealed more than the curves and fur of a young mate, that much he knew. Maybe Javen had been right when the old rat had mentioned retiring. It had been a joke, but maybe they should both have gone by now. If he had, then he wouldn't be in this mess now. And if Javen had, well... maybe if he was one to keep his nose down and keep himself to himself, he would have been okay too. But as it was, Javen was the Critters' Hero, the dog killer, and many more claims to fame. He wouldn't sit back and see Mariuz bring the Dell down. Not like Albrus. That was why he had to go.

A little rain had started, nothing more than a drizzle, but it nonetheless made the evening more unpleasant. He looked about at the others crouched in the nettles across from the bar. The Rat Guards were all youngsters, keen and ready to do their king's bidding. Art Sevrance, the psychotic weasel, was cleaning his claws with the tip of a dagger. His stomach churned at the memory of the Shredding of his one-time friend. He had wanted to stop it, to shout 'No!' and push the weasel away, but he would then have shared Javen's fate. Maybe several four-seasons ago, he would have done so, but now, he was so far under Mariuz's claw.

A Rat Guard hollered from the far side of the nettle lane. The wind had got up and the words were nearly drowned out, but the weasel laughed, popping the dagger back into its sheath.

"We've got him now. I was right, he wouldn't go straight away." He called his men together and they started to run off into the drizzle. When he realised that Albrus wasn't moving, the weasel stopped and called out.

"Have you seen enough blood, old rat?"

Far too much, thought Albrus. The weasel ran off, laughing and calling to his guards.

"A silver crown for the one that catches the traitor. If you leave him alive, that is!" Albrus watched as they darted into the undergrowth on the far side of the road, chasing their prey. He shook his head slowly. They won't catch him, he thought. Then he said it aloud.

"You won't catch him." He turned to face deeper into the undergrowth. "Because he is right here with me."

A figure stepped forward from behind a fallen log, a hooded cloak pulled up over his head and face. The cloak was heavily patched, and the different colours helped the figure blend in with the vegetation and underwood beyond. The tip of a silver tail protruded from under the hem of the cloak.

"That's right, Albrus." The figure whispered, his words barely carrying to where the old soldier stood.

"Hello, old friend." Albrus said, making no move for his

sword. He let the cloak slip open a bit, to show the newcomer his blade, and also the second scabbard on his other hip.

"Do not 'old friend' me. Does an old friend do this?" The figure raised his hands to his hood and pushed it back. A bloodied mess was revealed, the cuts to the ears still smarting and bleeding. The smur that seemed to hang in the air thinned the blood causing it to run in rivers down the face of Javen Silvertail.

"I had to. Don't you see. I had no choice."

"Just as I have no choice but to think of the critters that I serve. That we," he pointed to Albrus and then himself, "were meant to serve."

"You don't know what he is like…"

"I do. Which is why I am here, Shredded. What does Mariuz want from the Dell, Albrus. What is his final plan?"

"Whom do they chase?" Albrus ignored the question and nodded his head in the general direction that Art and his guards had taken.

"Someone in Brock's Bar told Johnny Lop-ear that his wife was ready to drop her litter. But the route to the door was blocked – and someone kindly offered him an open window, and a cloak not unlike one a King's Guard would wear."

"Johnny Lop-ear, you say? He's fast. I don't think they will catch him."

"And if they do track him, he lives the far side of the lake."

"Very good, Javen. Why aren't you over the borders by now. I know I would be. What do you want?"

The bloodied figure pointed to the sword on Albrus's hip.

"I have come for Thorn."

"The weasel will be upset when he returns from his wild rabbit chase, only to find out that my scheme worked and his didn't."

Javen pulled a thick bladed knife from his belt. It was no match against the length of a sword but was better than an open hand. Albrus nodded towards it, acknowledging the weapon.

"A barge knife, Javen. Do I need to see old Griswold after I deal with you? After all, consorting with a traitor is to sharein his crime."

"You leave the old fool alone, Albrus. He's only guilty for leaving his lockers undone and his tools strewn about his barge."

Albrus laughed, pulling his own sword from its scabbard. The rain was coming down faster and harder now, splashing on the ground.

"Intent on finishing the weasel's work, eh, old friend?" Javen retorted. His tone stabbed Albrus, reminding the old soldier of his betrayal. "You could always give me Thorn now and save us both the trouble. You know she will end up in my hand anyway."

Albrus leapt forward, closing the gap between them in the blink of an eye. His sword snaked out, intent on seeking out Javen's heart. The bloodied rat was just as quick. In the twitch of a whisker, he had sidestepped and parried, the thick blade clanking against the longer, but thinner sword. Albrus stood back, his free hand on his hip, his sword arm turned towards his opponent.

"You could always let me finish it and save us both the trouble."

"That does seem more trouble for me, so I will decline."

"Enough words, traitor! Now fight!" He lunged forward again, and once more Javen parried.

"Does that make it easier, old friend? Does it? You know in your heart that I am innocent."

Albrus snarled in response and darted in again for another attack. This time, Javen whipped his cloak off as he sidestepped, wrapping his opponent's sword arm with it. As he spun round, he flung the end of the cloak over Albrus's face, then kicked his knee. The old rat cursed, trying to free himself. Javen took advantage, driving his fist that gripped the hilt of his knife into Albrus's chest. Albrus went down with a curse, his arm still wrapped and trapped. Suddenly, Javen was upon him, pushing back down into the thick, worsening mud. Rain splattered all around and Javen struck him several times more. Finally, he leant down close to Albrus and whispered in his ear, the point of the knife held against his cheek.

"An eye for an eye, that is what they say, isn't it?"

"I didn't take your eye." spat Albrus, his snout covered in blood.

"No! But you took my ears, damn you!" Javen whipped the blade across the fallen rat's ears, slicing the tips off. Albrus shrieked in pain.

"Now we are both disfigured." Javen Silvertail smiled and smashed the hilt down on his opponent's head. The world went black for Albrus.

JAVEN SILVERTAIL STEPPED onto the riverbank, letting the small raft he had used to cross, drift away. Behind him was the Dell; the land and critters that he had sworn to protect. Now, he was exiled, but he would still fight for those critters. That was his way of life; to help those in need of aid, to draw a sword for those who couldn't, to bleed for those who had no more blood to give.

He tentatively touched his bandaged ears. The bleeding had finally stopped. His hand fell to the sword on his hip, the hilt a familiar feeling in his grip. He climbed the bank without looking back. He had no need. At some point, when he was ready, he would return to the Dell. He hoped then, to mete out justice to the foul beast that was Mariuz II. But for now, he was Javen Silvertail, outlaw.

ABOUT THE AUTHOR

Carl F Northwood was inspired by a misspent youth playing Dungeons & Dragons, and reading illustrious tomes detailing the deeds of heroes such as Fafhrd, the Grey Mouser, Conan, and many others. nNow he creates his own heroes and heroines, all eager to wield swords or mutter mysterious incantations at sinister villains.

He lives in a leafy coastal village in East Yorkshire with his partner, two of his five children, and many dogs and horses.

ALSO BY CARL F NORTHWOOD

The Maingard Chronicles

- Book 1: The Darkness Rising
- Book 2: The Demons Within
- Book 3: The Wheel of the Sun

THE DARKNESS RISING

An invading host appears in the skies above Maingard. Cities fall and the dark agents of the all-conquering Emperor work to subdue kingdoms from within.

Amid this chaos, a thief seeks a treasure and gains more than she bargained for. A refugee from another world brings warnings of the invasion. A Prince leads his forces to war. A bodyguard protects his wards with his very life. A soldier without a city yearns for revenge. A witch guardian seeks his spirit. And a Marshall seeks to protect the throne.

They all find themselves integral to the future of Maingard. Should they fail, then their world is doomed.

THE DEMONS WITHIN

Accompanied by Bev, Ishtara and Bryn Kar, Prince Garlen sets out to rescue his sisters. Will he be Garlen the Warrior, or Garlen, Lord of the Inns - as he is known to the citizens of Maingard. Meanwhile, Jerone Witchguardian tries to evade his pursuers in order to find what he seeks - his mentor, now reincarnated and reborn.

The future of Maingrd is on a knife edge as the invading host turns it attention to the West and to Tannaheim.

THE WHEEL OF THE SUN

A tale of returns...
As the city of Tannaheim slowly recovers from the Cassalian assault, Marshall Vent finds his plans interrupted by the arrival of the late Queen's brother, Lord Shales. A return that threatens the future of the Barstt line, especially with King Garlen missing, presumed dead.

Meanwhile Ingren also returns to Tannaheim, accompanied by Box and Ishtara. A homecoming that endangers all concerned.